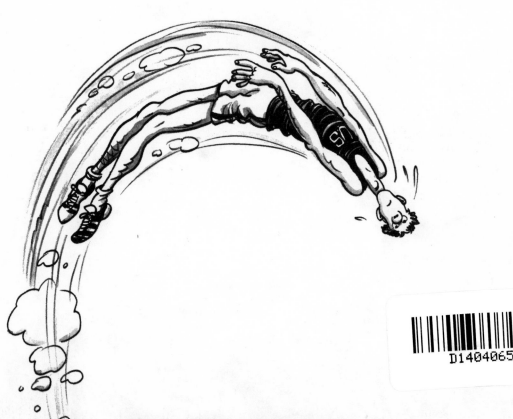

THE GIANT BOOK OF
MORE STRANGE
BUT TRUE
SPORTS STORIES

THE GIANT BOOK OF
MORE STRANGE

BUT TRUE SPORTS STORIES

by Howard Liss

illustrated by Joe Mathieu

Random House ⌂ New York

For my nephew, Steve Liss
—Howard Liss

For my dad, Joseph A. Mathieu
—Joe Mathieu

Library of Congress Cataloging in Publication Data:
Liss, Howard. The giant book of more strange but true sports stories.
SUMMARY: Describes true incidents from the world of sports—many humorous, all unusual.
1. Sports—Addresses, essays, lectures—Juvenile literature.
[1. Sports] I. Mathieu, Joseph, ill. II. Title.
GV707.L56   1983   796′.0207   82-13236
ISBN: 0-394-85633-3 (pbk.); 0-394-95633-8 (lib. bdg.)

Manufactured in the United States of America   1 2 3 4 5 6 7 8 9 0

CONTENTS

Baseball

Football

Boxing

Hockey

Basketball

Auto Racing

Golf

Tennis

Miscellaneous

THE GIANT BOOK OF
MORE STRANGE
BUT TRUE
SPORTS STORIES

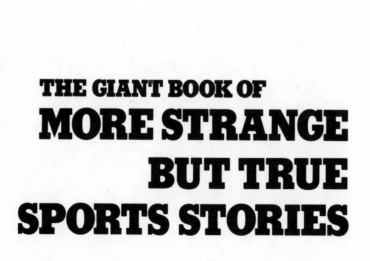

Sunglasses in the Snow

Jim Shrode, who played for Missoula, Montana, during the 1950s, was the only man to pitch a night baseball game wearing sunglasses. Once he wore the sunglasses at night during a snowstorm, which caused all sorts of difficulties.

Missoula was playing against Great Falls, Montana, and the snow that had been predicted began to fall before the game started. The Great Falls officials insisted that the game go on. The players weren't very happy, but there was nothing they could do.

Then the umpires halted the game because Shrode was wearing sunglasses.

"What's the difference?" screamed the Missoula manager. "Pretend they're ordinary glasses. We want to get out of here."

"We'll have to call the league president to get his okay," insisted one umpire.

"Because my pitcher is wearing sunglasses?" The Missoula manager almost had apoplexy.

While Shrode wore the glasses, the game went on. However, it was impossible to see a white ball coming through the swirling flakes, and in two innings the entire field was covered with snow. Finally the game had to be called off.

RAG-TAG HEROES

In amateur baseball the players do not get paid, but it still costs money to field a team. Someone has to pay for uniforms, bats, balls, and other equipment. When a team plays in another town, there are bills for transportation and meals. Sometimes it's hard to raise the money, especially when a team must travel a long way.

For example, when the Cincinnati team won the sectional championship of the Babe Ruth League in 1969, money was needed to send the youngsters to Morristown, New Jersey, where the championship playoffs would take place. Team manager Jim Kindt wrote to the Cincinnati *Enquirer* about the team's plight. Station WCPO-TV broadcast the item, and the money was raised.

Another team in need was the one from San Antonio, Texas. Many teams from various sections of the country went to New Jersey in airplanes. San Antonio's squad made the trip in a chartered bus, and the ride took 43 hours. Other teams had brand-new uniforms for the playoffs. San Antonio used the same uniforms they had played in all season.

In Babe Ruth League Tournament of Champions play, the rules call for double elimination. A team can lose one game and still remain in the tournament, but when it has lost twice, that's the end.

Cincinnati won its first game against Asheville, North Carolina, but then lost to San Antonio. Billy Daffin, the young Texas pitcher, defeated Cincinnati's Jim Dunway, 1–0. Later, Cincinnati lost to Puerto Rico and was eliminated.

San Antonio, the other "poor relations" team, continued to win. They beat Stamford, Connecticut, twice—once during the tournament and then again in the championship game. Billy Daffin was the pitching and batting hero of the playoffs.

The team that had straggled to New Jersey by riding in a bus for almost two days was the 1969 winner of the Babe Ruth League Tournament of Champions.

The Kicker

Percy Haughton, who coached football at Harvard, was a master of psychology. He believed that if a team *thought* they might lose, then they surely *would* lose.

In 1912 a young man named Charley Brickley earned a spot on the Harvard squad. Brickley was one of the finest dropkickers of his era, and coach Haughton devised a plan to beat Yale using Brickley.

In the past Harvard had never defeated Yale twice in succession and had never beaten Yale at Harvard Stadium. Haughton decided that 1912 was the year to end the jinx.

Just before his team took the field to warm up, Haughton brought two or three dozen footballs to the Harvard practice area. Then he told Brickley, "Kick those footballs over the crossbar from every angle. And don't miss."

As the Yale players watched, Brickley dropkicked every ball through the uprights. Never before had they seen such an exhibition. They were psyched out even before the opening kickoff. Brickley scored a touchdown and also kicked two field goals as Harvard won, 20–0.

A year later Brickley defeated Yale singlehandedly. He dropkicked field goals from the 35-yard line, the 38-yard line, the 32-yard line, and the 24-yard line. He also place-kicked a field goal from the 40-yard line. Harvard won, 15–5, defeating Yale for the second time in a row.

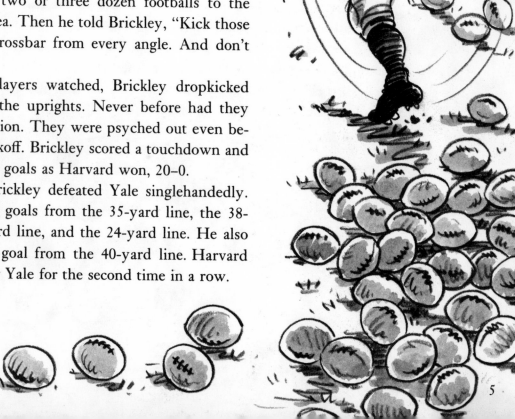

Not a Shot Was Fired

The sport of duck hunting has provided many a tasty Sunday roast for sharpshooters. In 1976 Dr. Ernest J. Fox, a veterinarian from Georgetown, South Carolina, went duck hunting at Annandale Plantation. With him was his friend Marshall Trueluck.

The two hunters set out their decoys and retired to their blind to wait. Sure enough, two ducks came winging overhead from opposite directions. They saw the decoys below and decided to take a closer look.

The ducks dived down, banged their heads together with great force, and fell into the water, dead.

Dribbling for Distance

In 1971 a fellow named Doug Melody, who played basketball for the University of Connecticut, scored a basket after dribbling a basketball for 65 miles.

Actually, Doug didn't go running back and forth on a court. He didn't even pound the pavement that far. There was no game in progress. The fact is that he started bouncing the basketball in Springfield, Massachusetts, while he was in the 2-foot aisle of a bus. The bus did all the traveling. After dribbling for one hour, fifteen minutes, and three seconds, he arrived at the campus in Storrs. Still dribbling, Doug went off the bus, into the fieldhouse, onto the basketball court (at last!), and stopped at the top of the key. Then he calmly swished the ball through the hoop.

Out for a Stroll

In 1867 a man named Edward Payson Weston made a bet of $10,000 that he could walk from Portland, Maine, to Chicago, Illinois. According to the rules of the bet, he had to cover the 1,326 miles in 26 days. He was followed by judges riding in horse-drawn carriages. Weston won the bet by taking 25 days and 22 hours, thus barely beating the deadline.

In 1909 Weston declared that he would walk from New York to California, a distance of 3,895 miles. He did it in 104 days. And then he beat his own record by walking back from California in only 77 days.

When he made his double cross-country hike, Weston was 70 years old.

NOT TO THE SWIFTEST

A rally is a peculiar kind of automobile race. It can cover a few miles or a few thousand. The course can be confined to one city or spread out over several countries. Unforeseen obstacles can include bad weather, road washouts, rock slides—sometimes even wild animals. Speed is not what's most important in a rally; accuracy and control are.

When plotting a course, rally officials decide on the exact amount of time it should take to cover the distance between two points. The car that comes closest to that time receives points.

Each car entered has two people, a driver and a navigator. The navigator is equipped with odometers, slide rules, and watches. He tries to time each leg of the rally. Often, however, almost all the instruments are useless. Breakdowns occur, or a car gets stuck in the mud. Local people are recruited to help push the car to solid ground.

A typical race of this kind was the East African Safari of 1963. The course would make an ordinary race driver seek another line of work. The rally took four days and covered 3,100 miles. It began in Nairobi, Kenya, and went through Tanzania and Uganda. The course led around part of Lake Victoria, over to the Indian Ocean, and back to Nairobi. The cars passed such exotic places as Mbale, Kampala, Meru, and Dar es Salaam.

On April 11, 84 cars started the rally. In one car, a Peugeot 404, were driver Nick Nowicki and navigator Paddy Cliff. They were the eventual winners.

About 250 miles from Nairobi, near Kakamega, all the cars had to get through a stretch of rain-soaked road that resembled a huge mud puddle. Paddy Cliff got out of the car and began to bounce on the rear bumper. His weight gave the rear wheels enough traction so the car could reach the edge of the road and slither through the jam of cars.

The Peugeot needed several pushes from spectators to get up Mount Elgon on the Kenya-Uganda border. To be sure, Nowicki and Cliff had to pay each pusher a few coins, but it was well worth the cost.

In a rally all local speed laws must be obeyed. Nowicki and Cliff averaged 53 miles an hour on the Nandi Hills Escarpment, but at the Nakuru control point, which had much better roads, the local speed limit was 30 miles an hour. To go faster would have cost the team 100 points.

In midrace the course had to be changed. A 90-mile stretch of road had been washed out by heavy rains. On and on sped Nowicki and Cliff, through fog, through rain, around boulders. Near the Morogoro Crater they saw herds of wild game. A tire blew out when they were doing 65 miles an hour.

In one area the road was completely under water. There was no way to tell how deep it was. They found out the hard way. Nowicki slammed the car into first gear and pushed through. The Peugeot slid and churned and finally made it to the other muddy side. At a different spot the same conditions were encountered. Nowicki edged the car into the water. He felt the floodwaters of the stream sweep the car sideways and immediately shifted into reverse gear. The car just made it to safety. Nowicki and Cliff found another place to ford the stream.

Uppermost in the minds of driver and navigator were hazards that they might not be able to evade. They knew that once a car going 70 miles an hour had been wrecked by smashing into a giant anteater!

Nowicki and Cliff beat their nearest rivals by 75 minutes. And they understood what *Time* magazine meant when it described the East African Safari: "If there were a Society for the Prevention of Cruelty to Automobiles, there would be no East African Safari."

I Dare You!

One of the toughest players in the early days of hockey was a man named Art Ross, who became a star just after the turn of the century. Ross didn't hesitate to battle a whole hockey team if he had to.

Because of penalties most of Ross's team was off the ice. Only he was left along with goalie Riley Hern. At the face-off Ross smacked his opponent across the hand with his stick, breaking the poor guy's thumb. Then he stepped back with a snarl, raised his stick, and stood over the puck, daring anybody to come and get it. Nobody did.

All Tied Up at the Moment

Sandy Valdespino was a fast outfielder who made it to the major leagues with the Minnesota Twins. When he broke into minor-league baseball, however, he had difficulty running the bases. He would try to steal every time he got on base, and sometimes he would fail to watch the coach's signals. As a result he was often picked off base, or he'd be tagged out trying for an extra base, thus killing a rally.

Finally his manager took drastic action. "Sandy," the skipper warned, "if you try any more silly base running, I'm going to tie a rope around you."

Sure enough, Valdespino ran through a coach's "stop sign" and was thrown out at the plate.

The next time Sandy got on base, the manager called for a time-out. He came off the bench carrying a rope. One end was tied around Sandy's waist; the other end was handed to the first-base coach. The crowd went wild with laughter, but at long last young Sandy Valdespino got the message.

Double or Nothing

Comedian Buddy Hackett is not only a very funny fellow, he is also an inventive practical joker. Often he gets his brightest ideas on a golf course. Buddy dreamed up one of his best brainstorms at the Sahara-Nevada Country Club in Las Vegas.

There is a water hole that has bedeviled Hackett every time he's played the course. The rotund comic once remarked, "On my better days I lose about fifteen balls in that lake." Hackett, who likes to make a few side bets, added, "All the wiseguys think I'm a patsy. They want to double their bets when we get to that hole."

One day Hackett was playing the course with one of the owners of the Sahara Hotel, where he was appearing. When they reached the water hole, the hotel owner selected his driver. Hackett, with a sneer on his lips, took out a pitching wedge, a club no golfer in his right mind would use.

"You're crazy," gasped the hotel tycoon. "I'll bet you a week's salary that you can't reach the green without using a driver."

Hackett then sprang his trap. "I guess," he said, "if I can get there without a driver, I'll get *double* salary. If I can't, I get *nothing*. Okay, it's a bet."

Then Hackett put a golf ball in his mouth, jumped into the lake, and swam across. No, the hotel owner did not pay off on the bet.

11

Those Amazing Globetrotters

In all countries where basketball is played, fans have flocked to see the Harlem Globetrotters perform their stunts. The team has drawn huge crowds in Germany, Russia, Canada, and various African and South American countries. Everyone has a marvelous time, laughing uproariously at the Trotters' antics. The Globetrotters don't play serious basketball, and nobody expects them to do anything but clown around.

However, once they were probably the best basketball team on any court, especially during the late 1940s and early 1950s. By then another great team, the Original Celtics, were only a dim memory for older basketball fans.

In 1948 the Minneapolis Lakers were the champions of the National Basketball Association. The Trotters, in spite of their clowning, were believed to be just as good. A game was scheduled between the two teams. It was hailed as "The Pro Basketball Game of the Year."

It was a tight contest. With just over a minute to play, the score was tied at 59–59. Marques Haynes then kept possession with his dribbling, driving the Lakers and the hometown fans to despair. At the last possible second he fired a pass to Elmer Robinson, who scored just a clock's tick before the buzzer. The Globetrotters won, 61–59.

The next year the teams clashed again. This time the

Trotters did a little more clowning, but they still won, 49–48.

All teams learned to respect the Harlem Globetrotters. Once a squad in Canada jeered at them for their antics, putting down their real ability. The Trotters gave them a lesson in manners, routing the upstarts, 122–20. Nor would the all-black Trotters let anyone get away with racist slurs. On one such occasion Al "Runt" Pullins was insulted and took matters into his own hands. For the rest of the game no Trotter except Pullins tried for a basket. He rang up 75 points, which was enough to win.

Once there was no room in pro basketball for black players, but in 1950 the Boston Celtics signed Chuck Cooper, a star at Duquesne. Then other blacks came flooding into the professional ranks. Players such as Bill Russell and Nat "Sweetwater" Clifton accepted less money from National Basketball Association teams in order to play in basketball's major league. It was good for basketball, but not so good for the game's most colorful team—the Harlem Globetrotters.

Now, although the Harlem Globetrotters can still play pretty good basketball, they are content to entertain their vast audiences with comedy routines.

A CENTURY OF FOOTBALL

In 1869 the first intercollegiate football game was played. By 1969 college football was 100 years old. The National Collegiate Athletic Association got busy with its calculators and arrived at some surprising numbers.

The officials figured out that in football's first century some 325,000 games had been played. About 900 teams participated, using approximately 2,500,000 players. The games were witnessed by about 750,000,000 fans.

1869 1969

13

What Are Friends For?

Ted Smith and Gordon Windhorn grew up together in Phoenix, Arizona. Both were interested in athletics. Ted was a pretty good sandlot outfielder and dreamed of a career in major-league baseball. Gordie was on the high-school track team, and he seldom played baseball. When he did participate in a game, it was usually softball.

One day Ted saw a newspaper story about the New York Giants conducting tryouts in Phoenix. Ted was eager to try out with the Giants, but he was shy about going to the field alone. He asked Gordie to accompany him.

"I'm not a baseball player," Gordie protested. "I don't even have a glove or a uniform."

"I'll lend you some of my stuff," Ted offered. "But please come with me."

"What position do I play?" asked the hesitant Gordie.

"Tell them you're an outfielder," Ted suggested.

"Okay," Gordie said, sighing. "I'm going to make a fool of myself, and I wouldn't do it if we weren't friends."

Once the boys were suited up, they trotted onto the field. Gordie went into the outfield. One of the coaches lifted a fly ball in his direction.

"Go get it, boy," called the coach.

Gordie went back, stuck up his glove, and the ball plopped into the pocket. He made several more catches, although sometimes he almost got his feet tangled. Mostly he reached the ball because he was so fast.

When it came time to swing a bat, Gordie surprised even himself. He smacked some line drives and hard grounders. A few of them would have been clean base hits in a real game.

Five youngsters were good enough to be signed by the New York Giants to play in their farm system. Ted Smith was not one of them. Gordie Windhorn received a contract. He was never a star, but he did make the major leagues. The boy who didn't think of himself as a baseball player went on to play for the Boston Red Sox, the New York Yankees, the Kansas City Athletics, and the Los Angeles Dodgers.

Relay

In 1979 Pope John Paul II visited the United States. Everywhere His Holiness went, he was greeted by huge, enthusiastic crowds. In Des Moines, Iowa, some 350,000 people turned out to cheer him. No vehicles of any kind were permitted to come close to where the Pope was. Yet the Des Moines *Tribune* managed to get out a special edition, complete with photographs, about an hour after the Pope had departed.

The *Tribune* had prepared for the event by recruiting 10 runners from the Ankeny High School cross-country team. Passing a package containing 241 rolls of film from runner to runner, the students relayed their cargo from the photographers to a waiting helicopter two miles away.

After that it was easy.

A Wizard with a Wrench

In 1903 several cars raced around a three-mile track at Grosse Pointe, Michigan. The winning car was a four-cylinder, 80-horsepower racer nicknamed 999. The driver was Barney Oldfield, who had been a bicycle racer. He became famous as a race driver. The man who built the car was a machine shop mechanic named Henry Ford.

The Greatest Comeback

It was February 1949. After participating in a tournament in Phoenix, Arizona, golfer Ben Hogan and his wife, Valerie, were driving home to Texas. Near a town called Van Horn, Texas, a huge bus went into a skid. There was no way to avoid a collision.

Instinctively Hogan threw himself over his wife to protect her. The move also saved his own life. The collision drove Hogan's steering wheel back against the seat where he would have been. Valerie Hogan sustained only a few small injuries. Ben took the brunt of the impact.

Hogan had suffered a double fracture of the pelvis, a broken collarbone, broken ribs, a fractured ankle, and severe internal injuries. For a brief moment Val Hogan thought her husband was dead. He lay with his head in her lap, pale and still. The doctors who sped to the scene must have thought Hogan was dead because they covered him with a blanket. Then Val Hogan heard a very faint groan. Her husband was still alive!

Hogan was taken to a hospital called Hotel Dieu, Hotel of God. There doctors worked around the clock for two days trying to patch him up. Just when they thought he was out of danger, he developed blood clots in his circulatory system. Surgeons operated immediately, tying off some of the veins in his legs. Later the doctors faced a battery of sportswriters and answered the barrage of questions.

Yes, the chances were that Hogan would live. Yes, he might be able to walk again, but perhaps not normally. No, there was no chance that he would ever play golf again.

For 58 days Hogan lay on a hospital bed, then he was sent home. It was then that the fighting spirit of "Bantam Ben" Hogan showed itself once more, as it always had on the golf course. He wasn't going to let a little thing like a cracked body stop him from coming back to the game he loved.

At first he was content to walk around his bedroom a few times a day. As time passed he walked around more and more. He did some exercises in spite of the pain. Slowly his muscle tone returned. By late summer he had begun to practice swinging a golf club. In December, just 10 months after he had almost been killed, Hogan was playing golf again. But he was still way off his game.

In January 1950 Hogan entered the Los Angeles Open. He shot a 73 in the first round, then fired three straight rounds of 69 to tie his old rival Sammy Snead. Hogan lost the playoff, but he had come back—partially.

Three months later Hogan entered the biggest, most important tournament of all, the Masters at Augusta, Georgia. Again he took a 73 on the first round, and in the second round he had a 68. The third round was almost too much for him but he managed a 71 to stay two strokes behind the leader. But his tired, aching body could not maintain the pace. He carded a 76 on the last round to finish tied for fourth place.

There was no stopping Ben Hogan after that. Two months later he won the U.S. Open. And in 1951 he won the Masters Tournament by two strokes.

Two years and two months earlier Ben Hogan had been presumed dead of injuries. Yet he came all the way back to win the coveted green jacket, the symbol of victory at Augusta.

BEAT THE CLOCK

On August 30, 1916, Winston-Salem and Asheville of the North Carolina League played one of the strangest baseball games on record. It was also the fastest.

When the teams arrived at the Asheville ballpark, Charles Clancy, the Winston-Salem manager, asked a favor of Asheville manager Jack Corbett.

"The last train for Winston-Salem leaves a little after three o'clock this afternoon," Clancy said. "If we don't catch that train, we'll have to stay over in Asheville until tomorrow. Can you help us out?"

It was Asheville's last home game of the season. Neither team was in the thick of the pennant fight, so the game really didn't mean much. Corbett agreed that game time could be moved up. Instead of starting at 2:00 P.M., the first pitch was delivered at 1:28.

Both teams hustled like mad. Every batter swung at the first pitch, which was always right over the plate. No sooner was the last out made in an inning than both teams were running to change sides. Sometimes that led to confusion. Once the Asheville pitcher delivered to the plate before his teammates could take the field. It was a clean single, but the Winston-Salem center fielder grabbed the ball and threw his own teammate out at second base. Whenever a player got a hit, he usually managed to get himself trapped between the bases and tagged out.

The game turned out to be something of a farce, but Winston-Salem did win over the regulation nine innings. The final score was 2–1.

At 1:59 the final out was made, leaving Winston-Salem ample time to make their train. It was the shortest game ever played, lasting exactly 31 minutes. Some fans who came to the game on time were surprised to find that it was already over.

Mr. L. L. Jenkins, the president of the Asheville team, gave a refund to anyone who wanted it.

Teenage Tennis Stars

The youngest woman ever to win the Wimbledon singles championship was Charlotte "Lottie" Dod. When she took the title in 1887, she was 15 years and 9 months old.

The youngest man ever to win the Wimbledon singles championship was Wilfred Baddeley. When he got his title in 1891, he was exactly 19 years and 175 days old.

The One-armed Major Leaguer

When Peter J. Wyshner was six years old, he fell off a truck. His right arm was caught in the spokes of a wheel and was so badly mangled that it had to be amputated a few inches below the shoulder.

The youngster had always loved sports, and he decided that he would participate along with other boys who had two good arms. He played football, basketball, softball, and other games, practicing constantly. He would wander down near the railroad that passed through his hometown of Nanticoke, Pennsylvania, and there he would toss small rocks into the air, hitting them deftly with a stick. Peter's father encouraged his handicapped son as much as he could. In time Peter's left wrist became extremely powerful.

When Peter's brother decided to become a prizefighter, he changed his name to Gray. Peter liked the name and changed his own to Pete Gray. He was determined to carve a career for himself as a professional baseball player.

In 1942, at the age of 25, Pete Gray was signed by the Three Rivers, Ontario, team of the Canadian-American League. Pete suffered a broken collarbone that year, but he recovered and went on to bat a rousing .381.

The following season he played for the Memphis Chicks of the Southern Association. In 1943 he hit .289, and in 1944 he raised his average to .333. But it wasn't only his hitting that earned so much respect for Pete Gray. He was truly a complete ballplayer.

He could run like a frightened deer. In 1944 Pete stole 68 bases. He stole home 10 times! In the field he could really go get 'em. Pete used a special glove with no padding. He would grab the ball, swiftly tuck the glove under the stump of his right arm, dig out the ball, and fire it back to the infield, all in one easy, fluid motion. That season 14

Southern Association sportswriters sent in ballots naming the league's Most Valuable Player. Pete Gray's name topped the list of players submitted by 12 of those sportswriters.

Pete was still playing during World War II. By 1945 the major leagues had very few good players, since most of the stars were still in the armed services. The St. Louis Browns of the American League decided to take a chance on Gray. They bought him from Memphis for $20,000.

Not only was Pete Gray a pretty good player by wartime standards, he was also a tremendous drawing card. Huge crowds turned out to watch this one-armed wonder in action. For example, despite bad weather, almost 40,000 fans came to see him play at Yankee Stadium. He drew a crowd of 65,000 in Cleveland. Whenever his name was announced, the fans gave him a standing ovation.

Pete didn't always enjoy good days, but every once in a while his bat came alive and he got plenty of hits. In a 1945 doubleheader against the Yankees, Pete got three singles and drove in a run as the Browns won the first game, 10–1. In that game he also went back to the wall to snare a long fly ball. The Browns won the second game too, as Gray helped himself to another single and a base on balls.

On July 4 Gray hammered out a double and two singles against the Philadelphia Athletics. Sportswriter J. Roy Stockton of the St. Louis *Post-Dispatch* wrote, "It was a great exhibition of courage, and you can use that word without restraint or blush, even in these war-torn days, when you sing of a gamester like Peter Gray."

Of course, Gray also made errors and lost some games for the Browns. Even he had to admit, "The pitching is a little too tough for me up there in the majors." He appeared in 77 games and batted only .218.

In 1946 the stars of baseball began to come home from the war and there was no longer any room in the majors for Pete Gray. He played in the minors for a while in Toledo, Ohio; Elmira, New York; and Dallas, Texas. In 1949 he retired from baseball.

Strangely enough, Pete Gray wasn't the only one-armed major leaguer. In the 1880s a pitcher named Hugh Daily played for Cleveland, which was then in the National League. During his career he won a total of 74 games, including 19 shutouts. One of those whitewash jobs was a no-hitter against the Philadelphia team.

Costly Card

Most youngsters know that baseball cards come in bubble gum packages. However, at one time they were given away by cigarette companies. In 1910 Sweet Caporal cigarettes offered cards with the picture of Honus "Hans" Wagner, the great shortstop of the Pittsburgh Pirates. Most of the Wagner cards have been lost, but about a dozen or so are known to exist.

One of those cards is worth more than $19,000 today.

Basket Bonanza

Englewood Cliffs and Essex were both junior colleges in New Jersey, but on January 20, 1974, they seemed to be in different worlds. Technically they were playing a game of basketball, but after a few minutes the game became an embarrassment. It was a horrible mismatch.

The first 26 points in the game were scored by Essex. That was merely a warm-up. By the end of the half Essex led, 110–29.

During the rest period someone on the Essex team mentioned the fact that the national scoring record in basketball was 202 points. They asked coach Cleo Hill if they could try to beat the record. Hill replied that he didn't think they could do it.

The Essex boys ran wild in the second half. Even the substitutes couldn't miss the hoop. The final tally showed Essex with 210 points, Englewood Cliffs with 67.

The statistics piled up by the Essex team were amazing. They scored on 97 out of 129 shots from the floor, 16 out of 22 foul shots, and took down a total of 89 rebounds.

THE HEIDI GAME

During the football season television schedules can cause headaches for the networks. Usually Sunday games are shown during the afternoon or very early evening. The rest of the night is prime time, when situation comedies, police shows, and network specials are presented.

What can happen when a football game runs too long? Does the show that follows have to wait for the game to end? Is the football game cut off and the new program begun? What do television viewers think? The National Broadcasting Company (NBC) found out on November 17, 1968. It was a lesson they never forgot.

The New York Jets and the Oakland Raiders were to clash in a very important game. It was scheduled to start at 4:00 in the afternoon. At 8:00 NBC was presenting the children's classic *Heidi*. Surely four hours was enough for any football game.

It was an exciting game, with the lead changing hands constantly. In the third quarter the Jets led, 19–14, but the Raiders rallied to take the lead, 22–19. Finally, with only a little over 40 seconds left to play, the Jets were ahead, 32–29. But Oakland was driving and had the ball on the Jets' 43-yard line.

At eight o'clock a commercial came on. Television viewers thought it was just another ad, since it was exactly 8:00. They waited patiently for the action to resume. One commercial followed another, which made the viewers unhappy. Then the ads were over.

What next appeared on the screen was a charming little 10-year-old girl named Jennifer Edwards who acted the role of Heidi. The children's special had begun. As far as NBC was concerned, the Jets-Raiders game was over.

Maybe the network thought so, but not New York fans. By the thousands the viewers began to call NBC; they called the newspapers; they called *everybody*. More than 10,000 calls flooded the NBC switchboard as enraged fans protested loudly.

Then NBC flashed "streamers"—bulletins—across the bottom of the screen. The first streamer gave a new score: Oakland 36, Jets 32. Moments later a new streamer gave the final score: Oakland 43, Jets 32.

Only when fans heard the nightly news or read the details in the newspapers the next morning did they find out what had happened during the last seconds of the game. A touchdown pass and the recovery of a Jets fumble had given Oakland two quick touchdowns and the victory.

All the executives at NBC offered different stories about the sudden change in programs. Nobody knew which story to believe. But the networks got the message.

Forever after, if a football game runs too long, the program that follows has to wait until the game is over. Rabid football fans usually get what they want.

Water Hazard

One of the strangest holes in golf is the seventeenth at the Players Club course in Florida. The green and the cup are situated on a small peninsula in the middle of a lake. The green can be reached by walking over a narrow causeway leading to it.

Some of the best golfers in the world have plopped balls into the lake trying to drop the ball onto that green. There is no fairway leading to the green, and no rough either. It's just water.

Nor will anyone go into the lake looking for golf balls. It is said that an alligator was seen floating around sunning itself.

Quick Hat Trick

In hockey, scoring three goals in one game is called "the hat trick." At one time the record for the fastest hat trick was held by Bill Mosienko of the Chicago Black Hawks. He got his trio of goals in exactly 21 seconds.

In January 1982 Steve D'Innocenzo of Holliston, Massachusetts, beat that record in a game against Westwood High School. He drove the puck into the net with 1 minute and 19 seconds to play. Six seconds later the young hockey player sent the puck past the goalie again. It took another six seconds for the third goal to hit the net. Total time elapsed for three goals: 12 seconds!

The Chief Fan

In 1906 a Sicilian nobleman, Count Vincenzo Florio, instituted an automobile race on his native island. It was called the Targa Florio. It was a twisting, rugged course, leading through the Madonie Mountains. Veteran drivers often talked about the Targa Florio. It wasn't so much the difficult course that drew their attention as much as one of the most interested spectators.

He was a bandit chief who lived in the Madonie Mountains. This chief led an army of about a thousand men. They preyed on travelers and farmers in the region. But they never once tried to stop a car.

Many drivers reported seeing the bandit chief. He sat on a hilltop, enjoying the race, cheering each car that passed. Finally he stopped watching the race. It was learned that he had been captured and shot.

The Underwater Marathon

It is difficult enough to swim the English Channel when conditions are perfect. It is an incredible feat to swim the Channel under water. Fred Baldasare, a 44-year-old frogman from Cocoa Beach, Florida, did exactly that using scuba gear.

Baldasare did not attempt the swim without some previous experience. He had tried twice before and failed both times. He had learned about the Channel and its currents. On July 11, 1962, he made a third attempt.

An underwater swimmer does not know where he is going. In order to maintain some sense of direction, Baldasare had someone in a boat topside tow a cage that he could follow.

A normal swim across the Channel is 22 miles. Since the currents kept tugging Baldasare north, he traveled about twice as far.

Baldasare started his swim off the coast of France. He reached the other shore, near the greens of the Royal Cinque Golf Course in Kent, England, exactly 18 hours and 1 minute later.

FATHER KNOWS BEST

Charles Lenglen was a wealthy Frenchman, and like all doting fathers, he wanted his daughter, Suzanne, to be accepted socially. He noticed that tennis stars who came to the Riviera were always well treated. Mr. Lenglen was determined to see his daughter become a tennis champion. He decided to teach her himself.

But Papa Lenglen knew little about tennis, so first he had to learn the game. He became a passable player. He also observed how the best players used their strokes. He borrowed their methods, imitating the service technique of one player, the backhand of another, and the forehand of someone else. He drilled his daughter in footwork and volleying.

Suzanne was only 11 years old when her father began to train her. Sometimes he would bribe Suzanne to keep the child on her toes. He would place a handkerchief on the court and offer her five francs if she could hit it with her serve.

Young Suzanne rose through the tennis ranks rapidly. From 1917 to 1926 she lost just one match, and then only because she was sick. From 1919 to 1923 she won the singles championship at Wimbledon. She defaulted because of illness in 1924, but returned to Wimbledon in 1925. It was then that Suzanne Lenglen played the kind of game that stunned the world of tennis.

She won both of the first two preliminary matches by scores of 6-0, 6-0. Neither of her opponents won a single game. In the quarterfinals her opponent fell, 6-0 and 6-0. In the semifinals the scores were no different.

In the finals she played Joan Fry of England. Fry won two games in the first set, but that was the best she could do. Suzanne won, 6-2, 6-0.

Suzanne Lenglen had won her sixth Wimbledon championship without losing a single set!

Klondike Contenders

In 1905 a team called the Ottawa Silver Seven was the champion of hockey. Since there was no National Hockey League then, any team could challenge for the Stanley Cup. A team from Dawson, Yukon Territory, in the heart of the Klondike area, decided to try for hockey's greatest prize.

In order to play, the Dawson team had to journey to Ottawa. It was a tough trip. The players traveled by dog team, by boat, and by train. All the travel was in vain. The Silver Seven trounced them twice. In the first game the score was 9–2. The second encounter was strictly no contest. The Silver Seven won, 23–2. Frank McGee, one of hockey's great all-time players, scored *14 goals*, a Stanley Cup record for a single game that will probably never be equaled.

Baseball's Craziest Race

During the winter of 1913–1914, John McGraw, manager of the New York Giants, recruited a group of major leaguers for an exhibition tour. One of the players was John "Hans" Lobert, probably the fastest base runner of his time. He had been clocked going around the bases in 13 4/5 seconds, which would be excellent time even today.

One day the teams played at Oxnard, California. Of course, touring teams were a great attraction and the stands were filled. Many fans were in the outfield, some of them local cowboys mounted on horses.

Before the game the mayor of Oxnard challenged Lobert to a race. "Who do I run against?" Lobert asked.

"How about racing a horse around the bases?" the mayor answered.

Lobert refused at first, but McGraw convinced him to go through with it. A lot of money was bet on the outcome. It was agreed that Lobert would run inside the base paths while the horse ran outside them.

Lobert got off to a fast start and beat the horse to first base. The cow pony was right behind him on the outside. Lobert gained speed rounding second, but the horse turned sharply and began to crowd into Lobert's area. Lobert was forced to break stride. Between third and home the horse passed Lobert and won the race by a nose.

Lobert wanted the horse disqualified for not living up to the rules of the race.

A Long Time Between Victories

The first intercollegiate football game was played on November 6, 1869, between Princeton and Rutgers. Rutgers won, 6–4.

One of the stars of that first game was a man named George Large. He almost ran himself ragged. Once Large and a Princeton player named Edward "Big Mike" Michael ran after a loose ball. Both hit a fence at the same time, knocking it down and spilling the spectators sitting on it. Large and Michael got up, took deep breaths, and went back to the game.

It took Rutgers 69 years to beat Princeton again in football. When they finally did, one of the Rutgers rooters watching the game was George Large. He was the last survivor of the first game, and the only player to see Rutgers beat Princeton twice.

Garbage Galore

The Indianapolis 500 auto race, held every Memorial Day weekend, is one of America's greatest sports spectacles. About 300,000 racing fans come to the track. Some sit in the stands. About 75,000 vehicles of all sorts drive onto the infield, and pretty soon the entire area resembles a huge cookout. Outdoor grills are unloaded from campers, vans, and station wagons and the smell of barbecue sauce is everywhere. Then it's over and everybody goes away.

What's left behind is about 6.6 million pounds of litter and trash. The race takes approximately three hours, but it requires 10 days to clean up the mess.

DETERMINED TO DIVE

Her name was Maxine Joyce King, but lots of people in her hometown of Pontiac, Michigan, called her Micki. There are many lakes in that region, and little Micki enjoyed water sports. Even at the age of four, she liked to climb up on her father's shoulders so he could toss her high into the air and she could flip over into the water.

At the age of 10 Micki joined the YMCA and saw a diving board for the first time. Testing the board, she felt almost as if she were leaping from her dad's shoulders. Micki began to take up diving in earnest. Along with other children she learned different kinds of dives. At the age of 15 she entered the Toledo YMCA meet and won. At 16 she entered the Olympic diving trials in Detroit but didn't do well at all. Still, she was learning, gaining experience.

Micki was at the University of Michigan when she came to diving coach Dick Kimball. She was still very green compared to other divers. Kimball encouraged her to work on the 10-meter platform (more than 30 feet high). Micki was just a bit scared, but she forced herself to climb that platform again and again. She improved tremendously. By the time she graduated in 1966, Micki had won three U.S. Nationals titles and the Canadian diving championship.

In 1966 Micki enlisted in the U.S. Air Force and graduated from Officers Candidate School with a commis-

sion as a second lieutenant. Then she was sent back to the University of Michigan to work with the Reserve Officers Training Corps. That was perfect, because she could also continue to study with coach Kimball.

Micki qualified for the 1968 Olympics. On the 3-meter board she went into a reverse one-and-a-half layout—a spring into the air, body straight; one and a half backward somersaults; and finally into the water, fingertips first.

Something went wrong. As she plummeted toward the water, her left forearm hit the board. She almost fainted with pain, but she tried her best to keep her arms straight. It didn't work. The judges saw what had happened.

The trainers applied ice to her forearm to stop the bleeding. Anyone else might have quit the competition right then, but Micki bravely tried to go through with it. But the agony was too much. Her final dive was terrible.

Micki wore a cast for four months, and after it came off she could hardly straighten her arm. It seemed that her diving career was over. But Micki loved diving and nothing could keep her away very long. Army officials granted her permission to participate in the World Military Games in Pescara, Italy. She was the first woman ever to compete with men in an international diving competition. It took time to work herself back into shape, but she managed to finish fourth in springboard and third in platform.

Finally, in 1972, Captain Micki King went to the Olympics in Munich. In the back of her mind was the memory of that dreadful, painful accident four years earlier. She could not bring herself to attempt that dive again. But there were others she could—and did—execute perfectly. Micki King was determined: she would *not* give in to fear of another accident.

Nothing could stop Micki in the 1972 Olympics. She won her coveted gold medal.

Later she became the first woman ever accepted as a faculty member of a military academy when she was named diving coach at the U.S. Air Force Academy in Colorado Springs. There she helped others overcome their fear of heights and compete in amateur diving.

Swish!

The date was April 6, 1935. At 7:00 in the evening Harold "Bunny" Levitt stationed himself at the foul line at one end of the basketball court in Chicago's Madison Street Armory. While some 4,000 spectators watched, Levitt began to pop in foul shots. He used the old-fashioned style of shooting—two hands on the ball and an underhand toss. It was almost midnight when he finally missed one. He had sunk 499 in a row.

The spectators thought Levitt was ready to quit, but he was far from finished. Once again he began to swish the ball through the net. By 2:30 in the morning he had sunk an additional 317 shots in a row. At that point the janitor told Levitt to go home because he was about to close the armory.

After that Bunny Levitt toured with the Harlem Globetrotters. There was a standing offer of $1,000 to anyone who could beat Levitt in a contest of 100 foul shots. Many tried, but no one ever got the best of him. The closest challenger sank 86 out of 100. Levitt's *worst* effort was 96 out of 100.

Yet Harold Levitt was never a star player, either in college or the pros. After all, he was only 5-foot-4.

The Hyattsville Mascot

Hyattsville, Maryland, is located near Washington, D.C. Back in the 1920s the Hyattsville public school baseball team had a possum as their lucky mascot. One day the mascot disappeared, and although the boys hunted everywhere, they couldn't find it.

At the same time the newspapers reported that a possum had wandered onto the White House grounds. President Herbert Hoover was fond of animals and adopted it. A photo of the possum was published in the local papers.

The Hyattsville boys were not sure whether the President had their missing possum and they wanted to examine the creature. A few of the boys went to the White House and asked to see the possum.

However, the possum was kept in the kennels and would not come out to be examined. All the boys could do was leave a note, asking for the possum to replace the one they had lost.

President Hoover, who loved kids (he later became chairman of the Boys Clubs of America), ordered the possum delivered to the Hyattsville team immediately.

The record shows that after recovering their mascot, Hyattsville's baseball team played in the Maryland state championship series. The possum had brought them good luck!

Anything for Charity

Some charities use cake sales or flea markets to raise money. The town of Portsmouth, New Hampshire, was the scene of a golf game to raise funds. It was called the Ceres Street Open.

Each player was permitted to use only two irons, a putter, and a tennis racquet. They all played with plastic balls.

The course was laid out through alleyways, along waterfront streets, and across parking lots. Golfers hacked their way into a restaurant lobby, phone booths, and garbage cans. Just for good measure, the course included an outdoor stairway and went through an old colonial house. Since the house was a historic structure, the players had to be careful of their shots.

The winner was a man named Ben Williams. His final shot was a putt that went into a drinking glass.

-FORE!

Yo-Yo

On December 2, 1950, Vic Toweel of South Africa fought Danny O'Sullivan of London for the world bantamweight title. Toweel knocked O'Sullivan down 14 times before the Londoner decided to quit in the tenth round.

THAT VALUABLE STANLEY CUP

In 1893 Baron Stanley of Preston, Canada's governor general, spent ten pounds (worth $48.67 in American money) to buy a silver trophy, which would be presented to hockey's championship team. The Stanley Cup has since become hockey's most treasured prize.

Over the years the Cup's appearance has been altered. The structure was changed, and that cost about $6,000. Engraving is also expensive. The cost of silver has skyrocketed since Baron Stanley first bought the trophy.

Of course, the honor that the Cup represents is priceless. However, a few experts have since estimated that Baron Stanley's purchase has increased in value to about $15,000.

The Shortest Home Run

In 1914 the Federal League was formed in competition with baseball's American and National leagues. Although the Federal League was considered an outlaw group, it was composed of many major leaguers who had jumped their teams for the bigger salaries offered by the new circuit.

All the rules of baseball were kept by the Federal League, except that they used only two umpires in a game—one behind the plate, the other stationed in the infield.

On a very hot summer day one of the umpires failed to show up for a game between Brooklyn and Chicago. Umpire Bill Brennan decided he might as well work the game by himself. He took up a position behind the pitcher's mound so that he could call balls and strikes as well as plays in the infield.

Brennan did fairly well for a few innings. However, every time he ran out of baseballs he had to trot into the home team's dugout for a new supply, and it was much too hot to move around so

much. Before the fifth inning began, Brennan got an armload of baseballs and made a nice pile of them behind the pitcher's box.

Then up stepped Brooklyn catcher Grover Land, who was not famous as a home-run hitter. Land got a pitch to his liking and drove a hard line drive that crashed into the pile of baseballs, sending them flying in all directions.

The Chicago infielders didn't know which ball Land had hit, so each picked up the first one that came rolling over. As

Land ran around the bases he was tagged by the first baseman, the second baseman, and the third baseman, but he ignored them all. When he reached home plate, the Chicago catcher also had a baseball and he tagged Land too.

Umpire Brennan didn't know which was the right baseball either. The only thing he could do was credit Land with an inside-the-park home run. Land's "homer" didn't travel more than 70 feet from the plate.

Warm-up for the Warpath

The full name of the school was the Indian Industrial Institute of Carlisle, Pennsylvania. It came to be known merely as Carlisle. Two immortals of football will forever be associated with Carlisle: Jim Thorpe, who played there; and Glenn Scobey "Pop" Warner, who coached there. The tiny school often tore up opposing football powers with great ease. In part it was due to the play of such great stars as Thorpe, Chief Redwater, Fraid-of-a-Bear, Little Boy Calac, and Black Bear. And Pop Warner was one of the great coaches of all time. He knew football. And he knew how to deliver a good, old-fashioned pep talk.

Once, before a game against favored Army, Warner really inspired his team. The sly psychologist said: "From the shores of the Little Bighorn to the banks of Wounded Knee Creek, the spirits of your people call to you. The men who died in Chief Joseph's retreat over the mountains, the Cherokees who marched on bleeding feet through the snow of their ancestral lands, tell you that you must win. These men [he referred to Army] are soldiers. They are the Long Knives. You are the Indians. Today we will know whether or not you are warriors!"

The Carlisle Indians took the field and overwhelmed the Army team from West Point by a big margin.

Busy Night

Preston Brown, a 125-pound boxer, thought he was pretty good with his fists. One night in 1913 he proved it. Brown was at the Broadway Athletic Club in Philadelphia when he announced that he would fight all comers, one at a time.

Six boxers accepted his challenge. Some were heavier than Brown. He knocked out the first five in early rounds and gained a decision over the sixth fighter.

Carrying On
the Tradition

Bill Vukovich began racing cars when he was 18 years old. He was reckless, often taking great risks during a race. He earned the nickname the Mad Russian because of the way he drove.

In 1952 Vukovich was leading in the Indianapolis 500 race with about 100 miles to go. The car's steering mechanism began to falter, and at last the steering column broke. Vukovich was forced to stop. As he watched the rest of the cars go by he said, "It's not hard to win here. All you've got to do is keep turning left."

Vukovich was back in 1953. It was so hot on the track that one of the drivers, Carl Scarborough, died of heat exhaustion. Vukovich won the race. He won again in 1954.

In 1955 Vukovich was leading again. He was almost a full lap ahead of all the others when suddenly driver Rodger Ward had an accident. His axle broke and he swerved out of control. The cars began to pile up. Driver

Al Keller tried to avoid Ward and sideswiped a car driven by Johnny Boyd. Vukovich was right behind those cars. Instead of "always turning left," Vukovich had to swerve to the right. His left front wheel hit Johnny Boyd's right rear wheel. Vukovich and his racer went up in the air and came down in an end-over-end crash. He was killed.

A driver who never won at Indianapolis was Melvin Eugene Bettenhausen. Everyone called the likable driver Tony. He was an excellent racer and twice won the United States driving championship. In 1955 Tony finished second at Indianapolis, and anyone who comes that close can be proud of himself. In 1961 he was at Indy again for the fifteenth time.

One of Tony's friends, Paul Russo, was having trouble with his car, but he couldn't figure out exactly what was wrong. He asked Tony to test it in a practice run. Tony was the kind of man who would do anything to help a fellow driver. He had the car going at full speed when it began to swerve and sway. A little metal cotter pin had been installed improperly. It fell out. Tony went into and over the wall, flipped over, and crashed. He died.

But racing is the kind of sport that gets into a whole family's blood. It's dangerous, drivers are killed, but that doesn't stop anyone.

In the 1968 Indianapolis 500, two familiar names were entered: Gary Bettenhausen, the son of Tony; and Billy Vukovich, Jr., the son of the Mad Russian.

JINX

Some pitchers can beat a team almost at will. Christy Mathewson of the New York Giants beat the St. Louis Cardinals 24 straight times, from June 16, 1904, to September 15, 1908.

By the same token, some teams can beat a pitcher every time they face him. From April 23, 1966, to July 24, 1969, the Chicago Cubs beat Don Sutton of the Los Angeles Dodgers 13 consecutive times.

They Shoulda Stood in Bed

When a country puts together an Olympic team, the best coaches and players are chosen. However, in the 1948 Olympics it was painfully obvious that no one in Iraq knew anything about basketball.

First the Koreans beat Iraq, 120–20. Then the Chinese beat Iraq, 125–25. The Iraqi team had lost each game by a margin of 100 points!

Has there ever been a basketball shutout in the Olympics? Yes, in 1936, when Czechoslovakia defeated Germany, 20–0.

The Longest Drive

The fifth hole of the Winterwood Golf Course at Las Vegas, Nevada, is par 4, a 450-yard layout. Par means the number of strokes good golfers take to get the ball from the tee into the hole. On September 25, 1974, Winterwood was the scene of the U.S. National Seniors Open Championship. One of the contestants was 64-year-old Michael Hoke Austin of Los Angeles. At 6-foot-2 and 210 pounds, he could hit a golf ball a long way. But even he must have been stunned by what happened.

Austin's tee-shot got caught in a 35-mile-an-hour tail wind. The ball bounced right on the green about a yard from the cup, but it kept rolling, finally coming to rest 65 yards past the hole. It was a 515-yard blast, the longest tee-shot ever recorded on a golf course.

The Shoeless Wonder

Abebe Bikila, the Ethiopian marathon runner, wasn't considered likely to win any medals in the 1960 Olympics. Ethiopia was not noted for its distance runners, and in the Olympic trials he had managed to finish only third. Besides, when Bikila lined up with the other 68 runners, the spectators saw that he wasn't wearing shoes. Part of the route lay over Rome's cobblestoned streets. What chance did a shoeless man have on such a roadway?

Before the race was over, the jeers had turned to cheers. The mobs along the route shouted encouragement to him and offered him water, which he refused. He won the gold medal, coming in 25 seconds ahead of the second-place finisher.

Bikila trained hard for the 1964 Olympics, but he didn't seem to have the same fire. As part of his training he entered the 1963 Boston Marathon and finished fifth. But he went to Tokyo in 1964, determined to do his best.

This time he wore shoes. Bikila took the lead early, and by the finish nobody else was even in sight. He won the race by more than 4 minutes.

Bikila tried again in 1968, but another victory was impossible. He sustained a small fracture in his foot and had to drop out about a third of the way through.

The Fargo Express

In the 1920s there was a prizefighter named Billy Petrolle. Because he hailed from Fargo, North Dakota, he was nicknamed the Fargo Express. Petrolle never became champion, but he had a good punch, he had courage, and he always obeyed his manager, Jack Hurley.

Petrolle got married, had a honeymoon, then went to New York to consult his manager about future fights. A movie called *The Big Parade* was playing at the Astor Theater on Broadway. Hurley bought Petrolle a ticket for $1.65.

That night a boxing match was scheduled in Newark, New Jersey, between Johnny Ceccoli and Ruby Goldstein. Goldstein was at the weigh-in; then, for reasons unknown, he took a train to California. A man named Laddie Rusy was the promoter of the fight. When he heard that Goldstein had left town, Rusy called Hurley. He offered $2,500 if Petrolle would fight Ceccoli. Hurley accepted. Then he went to the Astor Theater to find Petrolle.

When Petrolle arrived to see the show, he had just finished a huge spaghetti dinner. He had not been inside a gym to train in more than three weeks. And he had drunk a couple of glasses of wine with dinner and was feeling quite relaxed.

When Hurley mentioned the fight, Petrolle did not bother to ask about his opponent. He said, "What about the movie ticket? It's paid for."

"So what?" retorted Hurley impatiently. "Forget about the ticket. It cost $1.65. We're getting $2,500 for the fight."

Petrolle insisted that his manager get a refund. Then they took a train to Newark. Unfortunately, in the excitement of reaching Newark quickly, Petrolle discovered that he had brought two right shoes in his bag. A left shoe was borrowed. It was about three sizes too big, but Petrolle wore it anyway.

Although full of spaghetti and wine, and despite the facts that he had not trained for almost a month and was wearing a badly fitting shoe, Petrolle won the decision. As they were returning to New York, Hurley said, "I'll get you a ticket to *The Big Parade* for tomorrow."

"Okay," agreed Petrolle. Then he added, "Say, if you can get another bout for a good purse tomorrow, I can always skip the movie and see it some other time."

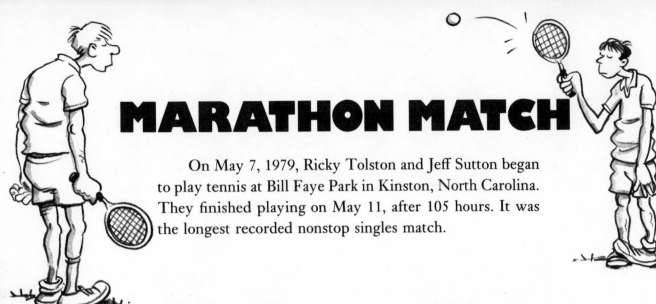

MARATHON MATCH

On May 7, 1979, Ricky Tolston and Jeff Sutton began to play tennis at Bill Faye Park in Kinston, North Carolina. They finished playing on May 11, after 105 hours. It was the longest recorded nonstop singles match.

The Banana Blade

When a hockey player uses a slap shot, the puck really zooms over the ice. Bobby Hull of the Chicago Black Hawks had a slashing slap shot. Once some measuring devices timed his shot at 110 miles an hour. Goalies insisted it was faster than that.

For a while part of Hull's fire power was due to his curved hockey stick. Many other players used a curved stick similar to Hull's. The shape came about by accident.

During the 1960–1961 season Hull's teammate Stan Mikita noticed that his shots and passes acted strangely. The puck seemed to rise, dip, sail, or curve in an arc. Mikita checked his stick and saw that it was cracked and bent. When other teammates tried using that stick, they got the same results.

Several players began to experiment. Mikita didn't know how his stick had gotten into that condition, so it was decided to imitate the shape of Mikita's stick by shoving others under a door, bending them, and leaving them that way overnight.

Because of the way it was curved and bent, the new type of stick came to be known as a banana blade. Hull and Mikita were outstanding shooters before the banana blade, but with the bent stick they combined to win the scoring championship six times. In 1968–1969 Hull scored 58 goals, which was then the record for a single season.

Goalies began to complain about the use of these outlandish sticks. They were downright dangerous. As goalie Ed Giacomin remarked, "It's hard enough to stop the straight shots, let alone some of the crazy ones. You never know what to expect."

Some of the forwards using the sticks weren't too happy either. They couldn't control the puck on breakaways, and their passes were often off target. Besides, because of the shape of the stick, it was almost impossible to try a backhand shot. The puck might end up anywhere at all.

Hockey officials realized that the banana blade was not good for the game. The offense had too much of an edge over the defense. The amount of curve in the blade was reduced drastically.

Today the curve or "bow" of a stick is under very close scrutiny by officials. If a player is caught using even a fraction too much, the result is an automatic two-minute minor penalty. Besides, today's hockey players don't need such an advantage. Wayne Gretzky of the Edmonton Oilers scored 212 points in the 1981–1982 season, and he didn't need a banana blade to do it.

Fishing for the Record

In 1976 Daniel Tveit of St. Paul, Minnesota, entered the St. Paul Winter Carnival ice-fishing competition. About 6,000 other fishermen also entered. Tveit won by landing a 3-pound, 7-ounce northern pike. Daniel, age seven, became the youngest fisherman ever to win the competition.

Wrong-Way Goal

In February 1982 Dwight Anderson of the University of Southern California scored one of the strangest goals in basketball history.

A University of Washington player had missed a shot at the basket. One of Anderson's teammates snared the rebound and fired the ball upcourt. Anderson raced after the ball, but by the time he caught up with it, he was almost out of bounds.

As his momentum carried him over the back line, Anderson flipped the ball over the *back of the backboard*. The ball swished through the net.

The basket counted because Anderson's feet had not touched ground even though his body was out of bounds.

The Switchers

All baseball fans know about switch hitters. As a general rule, left-handed batters can hit right-handed pitchers better than they can hit left-handed pitchers. That's because a lefty pitcher's curveball will break *away* from a lefty batter, and break *inside* to a righty batter. The same holds true for right-handed batters facing left-handed pitchers.

Down in the minor leagues during the 1920s, there was a young player named Paul Richards. He was one of the very few players in history who could throw equally well with either hand. However, since he was a shortstop, he threw right-handed.

One day Richards' manager had a problem with his pitchers. A couple of them were sick and the rest had been pitching almost every day. He asked Richards to pitch one game.

Richards disposed of the first two batters he faced. The next one was a switch hitter. Since Richards was pitching righty, the batter went up to the plate as a lefty.

After thinking for a minute, Richards put the glove on his other hand and went into his windup as a southpaw. Immediately the batter called for a time-out. Then he took his stance from the other side of the plate. Richards promptly put the glove back on his other hand. The batter stepped across the plate and got ready to bat from the left side again.

Both pitcher and batter kept switching until the umpire became dizzy. "How about it, boys?" he snapped. "Are you going to keep this up all day?"

"I can switch anytime I like," retorted the batter. "There's no rule that says I can't."

"That goes for me too," Richards insisted.

Finally Richards gave in. He decided to hurl the first pitch as a southpaw, the next pitch with the other hand, regardless of where the batter stood.

The count went to 3 and 2, and then the batter walked.

GOLFING DIET

Growing up in Jal, New Mexico, during the 1940s, Kathy Whitworth preferred sports to studies. She played softball, football, basketball, and even wrestled, mostly with boys. She held her own against them. But when she grew older and tried to keep on participating, the boys rejected her.

Kathy was a very unhappy girl. Instead of being active, she stayed at home doing almost nothing. Then she began to eat, not just at mealtime, but between meals as well. She craved chocolate milkshakes and desserts. Kathy Whitworth got *fat*. Her parents tried to put her on a diet, but it was useless. By the time she was in high school, she weighed about 250 pounds and was 5 feet 9 inches tall.

She tried tennis, but that was a disaster. Although other teenagers were swift and graceful, Kathy could scarcely lumber after the ball. She realized that her peers were laughing at her. Doctors warned her that obesity was harmful to her health.

Kathy tried her best to diet, but it was difficult. Then one day she went to a golf course with some friends. She tried to play, and although she wasn't very good at first, she liked the game. Kathy started playing as often as possible.

Her whole life changed. At first she taught herself the stances and swings, but then she realized she needed help. Kathy turned to Hardy Loudermilk, the Jal Country Club golf pro. Loudermilk saw Kathy's potential and began to train her. But that was not the only benefit for Kathy. In a year, because she was exercising and no longer sitting at home, she had lost 50 pounds.

Kathy's next golf teacher was Harvey Penick, and he thought she might become a champion golfer. Penick was in Austin, Texas, so Kathy and her mother often made the 400-mile trip by bus. Penick worked with his young pupil constantly. And Kathy lost 25 more pounds.

When Kathy graduated from high school, she entered the New Mexico State Amateur, her first big tournament. She won, making her the girls' state champion. She won the tournament again in 1958.

Soon afterward Kathy Whitworth turned professional. She was only 19 years old. She didn't suddenly catch fire and become an overnight sensation, but she did begin to be noticed by other women golfers. As her earnings went up her weight came down, dropping to 140 pounds. And by the end of 1973 she had won a record-breaking $488,319 as a tournament player.

Kathy took her success modestly. She often told her friends, "If it wasn't for golf, I'd probably be the fat lady in the circus now."

King of the Ring

Professional wrestling today is more show business than sport. Most modern wrestlers would have been disqualified immediately if they had used their "normal" tactics in the old days, before television made the sport so popular.

Many years ago a young boy named Robert Friedrich got his hands on a 50-cent mail-order book about wrestling. The book had been written by a man named Evan Lewis. At the age of 14, young Robert decided to become a professional wrestler. In order to keep his parents from finding out, he changed his name to Ed Lewis, after the man who wrote the instruction book.

During his career he developed a punishing headlock, and so he was given the nickname Strangler Lewis. By July 4, 1916, he was ready to challenge the champion, Joe Stecker. The fans in the Omaha arena watched Stecker and Lewis wrestle for five and one-half hours. Finally the match was called a draw. In 1920, Lewis and Stecker met again for the championship at the 71st Regiment Armory in New York. Lewis won.

Strangler Lewis wrestled all comers for 43 years. In 6,200 matches he lost only 33. Once he challenged heavyweight boxing champion Jack Dempsey. Dempsey would box; Lewis would wrestle. Dempsey refused the offer. After all, Lewis weighed about 260 pounds and had a chin like granite.

Ed "Strangler" Lewis was probably wrestling's greatest champion. And he first learned about the sport from a half-dollar mail-order book.

Low Scorers

In 1968 Carl Yastrzemski won the American League batting championship with an average of .301. Nobody else in the American League that year even reached the .300 mark.

The First Pro Football Game

Pro football was actually born on August 31, 1895. A team from Latrobe, Pennsylvania, played against a squad from nearby Jeanette. A fellow named John Brailler (who later became a dentist) was paid 10 dollars to quarterback the Latrobe team. It has never been established how much the other players were paid.

Latrobe won, 12–0.

The Skill of an Old Pro

Juan Manuel Fangio was one of auto racing's greatest drivers. The record book shows that he won the World Champion Driver title in 1951, then again in 1954, 1955, 1956, and 1957. It was not merely because he drove such outstanding cars as a Maserati, Mercedes-Benz, and Lancia Ferrari, but more because he was incredibly skilled behind the wheel. And Fangio was smarter than his rivals. He planned a race down to the last detail. In the 1957 Nurburgring race, he needed all his skill to win because of an inept pit crew.

Fangio was 46 years old then, driving a Maserati. His toughest opponents, he realized, would be 27-year-old Peter Collins and 28-year-old Mike Hawthorn, both driving Ferraris. They had the youth and stamina to withstand the rug-

ged 14.2-mile course with its 174 curves, steep drops, and bumpy paving. A driver had to go around the track 22 times to finish. But Fangio was confident because he had a plan.

He knew his Maserati was lighter than the Ferraris. Fangio planned to carry only half a tank of fuel, while the other cars carried a full tank. Fangio would save time because his lighter car would go faster. On the other hand, Collins and Hawthorn wouldn't have to stop for fuel but Fangio would. However, if he had enough of a lead, Fangio could get away quickly after his pit stop without losing too much time. By then the Ferraris' tires might not be in good shape. So Fangio instructed his pit crew to be ready with two rear tires for quick changing.

As was expected, the first three laps saw the three favorites grouped together. On the fourth lap Fangio edged ahead. His lighter car was simply too fast for the others, and his experience enabled him to cut split-seconds from the stopwatch. By the time the race was half over and Fangio went into the pit, he had a 28-second lead over Hawthorn.

Fangio got out of the car and the mechanics went to work. But it was taking too long—much too long. "Hurry up!" Fangio called impatiently.

The seconds ticked by . . . 40 . . . 45 . . . 50 . . . At last Fangio was back in the car and racing, but it had taken 53 seconds! He was a full 50 seconds behind both Collins and Hawthorn because his pit crew seemed all thumbs.

Now Fangio seemed hopelessly behind, but he began to use all the tricks he had learned over long years of racing. He took chances. Where some curves should have been taken at 94 or at most 95.8 miles an hour, Fangio roared into them at 95.6—just short of the maximum, but also slightly faster than his rivals. Each tenth of a second saw him gain ground.

By the sixteenth lap he was 33 seconds behind; by the eighteenth he was 26 seconds behind. And still Fangio kept coming. By the start of the twenty-first lap Hawthorn had a lead of only 2 seconds, with 2 laps to go. Then came a curve. With his wheels cutting into the grass at the edge of the pavement, Fangio shot past Hawthorn, and then he drove with magnificent control over the final lap, taking the checkered flag and winning by 3.6 seconds.

Perhaps Fangio realized he was getting too old to continue racing. Or maybe the clumsiness of his pit crew was more than he could bear. That German Grand Prix race at Nurburgring was the last one for the great Juan Manuel Fangio. He retired afterward.

The next year the winner of the World Champion Driver title was the man he had defeated in his last race, Mike Hawthorn.

THE WONDER TEAMS FROM PASSAIC

Perhaps it was the good coaching that made the basketball team from Passaic (New Jersey) High School so great. Their skipper was Professor Ernest Blood, who had begun playing basketball in 1892, only a year after the game was invented. He began coaching in New England where he was born, then moved to Potsdam, New York, where his high-school team never tasted defeat. That particular winning streak lasted from 1906 through 1915.

Then Professor Blood moved to Passaic. There he began to recruit the best players from the city's 12 schools.

Even though Blood wasn't a young man, he taught basketball by example, not by giving orders. He often put on a uniform to work out with the boys.

Starting in 1915, Passaic High won 41 straight games before losing the New Jersey state championship game in 1919. The team promptly resumed its winning ways starting in 1920. Beginning with a 44–11 victory over Newark Junior College, Passaic High rattled off 26 straight victories. On and on went the streak: 31 straight wins in 1921, 33 straight in 1922, 28 in a row in 1923, another 29 straight in 1924, then 12 more in a row in 1925. All in all the Passaic "Wonder Teams" ran off a string of 159 consecutive regular-season victories.

But nothing lasts forever. On February 6, 1925, Hackensack (New Jersey) High School finally dropped Passaic, 39–35.

Professor Blood had already left the school after the 1923–1924 season. However, the record he set will probably never be equaled by another boys' high-school team. From 1906 through the 1923–1924 season Ernest Blood's teams lost only one game to another high school!

As great as Passaic's record was, a far more impressive record was set by the girls' varsity team from Baskins (Louisiana) High School. Starting with the opening game in 1947 against Ogden High, Baskins won 218 straight regular-season games, a streak that lasted into 1953.

Baskins' coach was Willie Edna "Tiny" Tarbutton. In her first nine seasons at the head of the girls' team, Tiny's squads won the championship eight times.

One for the Gipper

In his years as a movie actor, President Ronald Reagan made many pictures, but one of his most popular roles was that of George Gipp, the Notre Dame football star of 1919–1920. The part of the movie that caused many viewers to cry was the deathbed scene. Gipp lay dying on a hospital bed while his coach, Knute Rockne (played by Pat O'Brien), listened to his last words.

George Gipp was truly an outstanding athlete. He could run swiftly and was a great receiver. In one game against Army he gained 124 yards from scrimmage, ran back kicks for 112 yards, and caught passes for 96 yards. In that game

he had a total of 332 yards gained. Gipp could also boot the ball. In a game against Western State Normal, he dropkicked a 62-yard field goal, which was only one yard short of the record.

The Gipper was also a fine baseball player. He was offered a contract by the Chicago Cubs of the National League.

In November 1920, after playing against Northwestern, Gipp complained of dizziness and fever. He had pneumonia and was taken to the hospital. There was no way the doctors could save his life, since miracle drugs like penicillin had not yet been invented.

On December 14 Gipp was visited

by coach Rockne. The words he spoke might well be considered corny, perhaps invented by a Hollywood screenwriter. But Gipp did speak them.

"I've got to go, Rock . . . it's all right, I'm not afraid. . . . Sometime, Rock, when the team's up against it . . . when things are wrong and the breaks are beating the boys . . . tell them to go in there with all they've got . . . and win one for the Gipper. . . . I don't know where I'll be, Rock . . . but I'll know about it . . . and I'll be happy."

On November 10, 1928, Notre Dame played Army, which was undefeated. Notre Dame, on the other hand, had won four games and lost two. More than 85,000 fans jammed Yankee Stadium in New York to watch these traditional rivals go at it. At halftime the score was deadlocked at 0–0. However, Notre Dame seemed worn out.

As a rule, Knute Rockne gave his team a pep talk between halves. This time he didn't. Speaking softly, he told of George Gipp's final moments of life. The locker room was still as Rockne came to Gipp's dying words: "When the breaks are beating the boys . . . tell them to win one for the Gipper."

The second half proved to be an exciting 30 minutes of football. Army took a 7–0 lead, but Notre Dame came back to score two touchdowns. Both extra points were missed, and the Fighting Irish led by 12–7. Army fought hard. Led by All-American halfback Chris Cagle, nicknamed the Gray Ghost, Army brought the ball all the way to Notre Dame's one-yard line when time ran out.

Notre Dame had scored a great upset. The team was looking forward to the following Saturday when they played at home, in South Bend, Indiana. Notre Dame had not lost a home game since 1908. Their opponent was a mediocre Carnegie Tech team.

Carnegie Tech upset Notre Dame, 27–7.

Ancient Aggies

When boys and girls kneel down to shoot marbles, they may not know that marbles is one of mankind's oldest sports. The game is thousands of years old. Marbles have been found in the tombs of Egyptian pharaohs and in the graves of American Indians.

The first marbles were made of stone, polished wood, and even the knucklebones of sheep. In the years that followed, marbles were made of glass, agate, marble, brass, and steel.

Gloves

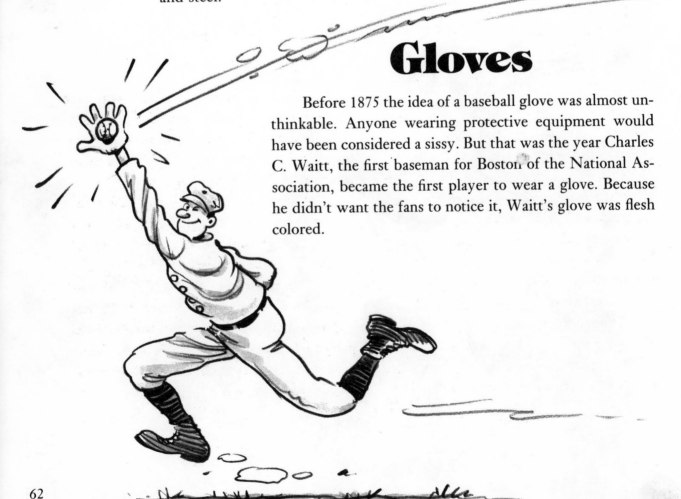

Before 1875 the idea of a baseball glove was almost unthinkable. Anyone wearing protective equipment would have been considered a sissy. But that was the year Charles C. Waitt, the first baseman for Boston of the National Association, became the first player to wear a glove. Because he didn't want the fans to notice it, Waitt's glove was flesh colored.

Scouting the Kids

In the spring of 1960 several officials of the Boston Bruins hockey team made a trip to a town called Gananoque in Ontario, Canada. They had gone to see the All-Ontario Championship Tournament played by kids in the Bantam Division. Bantams are barely into their teens. The Boston officials had heard about a couple of youngsters who showed promise, and they wanted to scout the boys for future consideration.

For a few minutes the Boston officials watched the two boys they had come to see, but they soon turned their attention to a player on the Parry Sound team. He wore number 2 and played defense. The scouts could hardly believe their eyes. Although the boy was only 12 years old and smaller than most of the others on the ice, he was skating rings around everybody. He always seemed to have the puck and he was always a step ahead of the other boys. The officials were amazed. The youngster also had extraordinary stamina. He played for 58 of the game's 60 minutes, leaving the ice for 2 minutes because of a minor penalty. Parry Sound lost, 1–0, but number 2 won the trophy for Most Valuable Player in the tournament.

Of course, the Bruins could not sign a 12-year-old boy, but they wanted to make sure they would have a chance to talk to his parents. They decided to "sponsor" the Parry Sound team. In those days sponsors paid for a team's equipment. The parents were usually so grateful that they signed with that team when the boy came of age.

Eventually the Bruins did sign the youngster from Parry Sound. He went on to star in Junior hockey, and when he was 18 years old he joined the Bruins.

His name was Bobby Orr. Almost everybody agrees that he was the finest defenseman ever to play in the National Hockey League. The Boston scouts knew he would be a superstar when Bobby was only 12 years old!

PRETEEN PINCH HITTER

At the age of twelve Joey Relford became the youngest player ever to participate in a minor-league baseball game.

Relford, a black youngster, was the batboy for the Fitzgerald team of the Georgia State League. Minor-league baseball was still for the most part segregated, and blacks and whites played in separate leagues. The Georgia State League was all white. On July 19, 1952, Fitzgerald was losing to Statesboro, 13–0, and by the eighth inning the fans had grown restless.

"Put in the batboy," they shouted.

Fitzgerald manager Charles Ridgeway heard the fans yelling and decided to give them what they wanted. He talked to umpire Ed Kubick, who said it was okay to put young Joey into the game. The boy was sent up as a pinch hitter and hit a hard grounder to third. He was thrown out at first base.

Then Joey went out to play center field, where he handled himself very well, making a fine catch of a line drive.

Officials of the Georgia State League were extremely displeased with the incident. The next day umpire Ed Kubick was fired and manager Charles Ridgeway was fined and suspended. As for Joey Relford, he had become the first black "player" to take part in a Georgia State League game. A few days later he lost his job as batboy.

Quick Kayo

When welterweight boxers Bob Roberts of Nigeria and Teddy Barker of England clashed in Maesteg, Wales, it turned out to be a very brief encounter.

No sooner had the bell sounded than Roberts shot out of his corner. As Barker came in, Roberts swung a wild right. Barker ducked and came up with a short right that found its mark on Roberts' chin.

Roberts went down, but he got up almost immediately. However, the referee saw that Roberts was completely dazed—in boxing jargon, he was "out on his feet." The referee stopped the bout and awarded it to Barker on a technical knockout.

From the opening bell to the end of hostilities, only 10 seconds had passed. It was the shortest fight on record.

What a Riot!

Many fans tend to worship star athletes. The Montreal Canadiens' rooters loved their star wingman, Maurice "Rocket" Richard. In their eyes that hockey player could do no wrong. If he got into a fight, naturally the other person was at fault. At least that was how they felt.

On March 13, 1955, Richard got into a fight that had a direct bearing on the National Hockey League championship. The Canadiens led by four points in the standings with only four games left to play. It seemed certain they would beat out their nearest rivals, the Detroit Red Wings.

Playing against Boston, Richard was high-sticked by Hal Laycoe. Richard suffered a scalp cut that later required eight stitches. The enraged Richard went on a rampage. He broke his hockey stick across Laycoe's back, then turned on Cliff Thompson, one of the officials, and punched him in the jaw.

Had the fight been confined to Richard and Laycoe, both would have received penalties and the incident would have been closed. But *nobody* is permitted to strike an official in *any* sport. National Hockey League president Clarence Campbell suspended Richard for the rest of the season, including the playoffs.

The suspension cost Richard the scoring championship. His teammate "Boom Boom" Geoffrion won it.

66

Strangely, the fans booed when Geoffrion won the honors. He couldn't understand why they felt that way. After all, he was a star with the Canadiens too. But the fans weren't finished showing their anger yet.

When the Red Wings next came to Montreal to play, the Forum had 200 police on duty to handle the crowd. When Clarence Campbell walked in, one fan came up to him as if in friendship. He stuck out his hand. When Campbell put out his own hand for a handshake, the fan punched him.

Almost immediately a riot broke out. A smoke bomb went off and the ice was showered with debris. When Campbell forfeited the game to Detroit, it was more than the fans would accept. The riot flowed out into the streets. There were looting of stores, fistfights, and overturned automobiles. It was a city-wide reign of terror.

The only person who could stop the riot was Rocket Richard himself. He went to a radio station, took over the microphone, and pleaded with the fans to calm down and go home. He admitted that the fight on March 13 had been mostly his own fault, and he would accept his suspension like a man. Gradually the rioters ceased their destruction and left the streets.

The Canadiens not only lost their lead, they also lost in the Stanley Cup finals.

They Minded Their Manners

When the first Wimbledon tournament was held in 1877, the players had a very strict code of ethics. It wasn't important who won, as long as the tennis match was fair. That meant nobody had to work very hard or move around too much.

The ball was served underhand. The receiver didn't attempt a hard return; he simply looped it back over the net. A backhand return of serve was seldom attempted. Causing an opponent to run after a ball was considered unfair, ungentlemanly. One tried to hit the ball where his opponent could reach it. Tennis, after all, was a polite game, a bit of exercise. Rushing the net was poor form.

When someone did fail to return the ball, he would exhibit excellent sportsmanship and call out, "I say, jolly good stroke, old top."

Twenty-two players entered that first Wimbledon. One was a man named Spencer Gore. He had no patience with the kind of foolishness practiced by the others. To him, the basic idea of tennis was to win the game, to keep his opponents from returning the ball.

Gore disposed of the opposition in a businesslike manner. He didn't do anything as crude or caddish as smash the ball hard. He would have been considered a blighter, an oaf, a boor. He did rush the net and volley before the ball could bounce. His gentle taps were placed so that his opponents could not reach them.

The losers accepted defeat gracefully, but then tried to have the no-bounce volley outlawed. But the rules dictated that such volleys were permitted, and there were no changes in spite of the protests.

The Longest Basket

On January 16, 1970, Steve Myers of Pacific Lutheran University took a shot at the basket. What made the attempt so strange was the fact that Myers was standing out of bounds behind his own end line. The ball arced up and dropped into the net like a homing pigeon. Later the shot was measured at 92 feet, 3½ inches.

Of course, the basket was illegal, but the crowd shouted its approval. The officials gave in and let the points count.

VERSATILITY

Many baseball players can play more than one position, particularly utility men. These valuable substitutes are sometimes called on to play second base, third base, shortstop, or even the outfield. In 1965 Bert Campaneris of the (then) Kansas City Athletics played *all* the positions, and he did it in a single game.

Attendance had fallen off badly, and club owner Charley Finley dreamed up the gimmick in order to draw fans to the ballpark. He even took out a million-dollar insurance policy on Campaneris to dramatize the event.

Campaneris, normally a shortstop, opened that game against the California Angels playing his usual position. In the second inning he played second base, in the third in-

ning he went to third base, and then went to the outfield for innings four, five, and six. He played first base in the seventh, pitched in the eighth, and caught in the ninth.

In the final inning, while Campaneris was behind the plate, the Angels tried a double steal. Ed Kirkpatrick, a big 200-pounder, was on third, and he came steaming home. Campaneris took the throw and held on while Kirkpatrick bowled him over. After tagging Kirkpatrick, little Campy tried to fight with the bigger man. The insurance company was probably somewhat frightened by the collision, but Campy wasn't hurt.

In 1968 Cesar Tovar of the Minnesota Twins matched the nine-position feat. The team Tovar faced was the Athletics. Tovar started out by pitching, and the first man he faced was Bert Campaneris!

Death of a Mare

Empress Bullet, a light-gray five-year-old mare, never amounted to very much as a racehorse. In 1981 she was entered in 19 races and won only once. On January 18, 1982, she was entered in the $22,000 Whitestone Purse at Aqueduct Race Track, New York. It was the fiftieth—and last—race of her life.

Shortly after the race began, Empress Bullet threw her rider, Amado Credido, Jr. The jockey wasn't hurt. The riderless horse continued the race as she had been trained to do.

At the first turn Empress Bullet drew even with Storm Petrel, the lead horse. Gregg McCarron, Storm Petrel's jockey, realized that Empress Bullet might swerve into the other horses. He reached out and tapped Empress Bullet on the mane to steady her. Later, in the home stretch, he nudged her with the whip again.

Without the weight of a rider, Empress Bullet pulled away and crossed the finish line first. Of course a horse without a jockey cannot win a race. Storm Petrel was declared the winner.

But Empress Bullet did not realize the race was over. She just kept running at top speed. An outrider chased the horse. He forced her to the outside rail, hoping that might stop her.

There was a gap in the metal railing where horses enter the track. With no rider to guide her, Empress Bullet appeared to panic. She ran right into the edge of the protruding railing. The metal pierced her heart and lungs. It was a fatal injury. The horse had to be destroyed humanely, with an injection.

Empress Bullet was not a great racehorse. But she always tried her best, with or without someone to show her the way.

Football Nicknames

All football teams have nicknames. For example, the Notre Dame team is called the Fighting Irish, the University of Southern California team is called the Trojans. The most popular team nickname in college football is Tigers. Twenty-seven schools are known to use it, among them Auburn, Louisiana State, Princeton, and Missouri. Next most popular are Bulldogs and Bears, with 17 teams each. After that come Wildcats with 16 and Eagles with 13.

Bad Hop Bonanza

While playing second base for Kansas City of the old Federal League, William "Duke" Kenworthy got in position to field a grounder, only to have the ball hit a big pebble and bounce over his head. Kenworthy picked up the pebble, examined it, and found that the little nugget was solid gold!

Taking Turns

Spartanburg County, South Carolina, was the scene of a strange basketball game in 1976. A girls' team from Mabry Junior High School took on a girls' team from D. R. Hill Junior High, and each team took turns dominating the other.

In the first half D. R. Hill scored 26 points while Mabry got nothing. In the second half Mabry racked up 28 points while D. R. Hill's score was zero.

The final score: 28–26, Mabry.

THE BIGGER THEY COME . . .

The boxing record book states that Robert Fitzsimmons was the heavyweight boxing champion of the world. "Ruby Robert," as he was called, won the title from James J. Corbett in 1897 and lost it to James J. Jeffries in 1899. Yet Fitzsimmons was not a real heavyweight (175 pounds or more). His usual weight was about 165 pounds.

On April 30, 1900, Fitzsimmons fought a man named Ed Dunkhorst in Brooklyn, New York. By then Fitzsimmons was 37 years old. His opponent weighed 305 pounds.

Fitzsimmons decided that he had to wear his man down. He made up his mind to dart in, throw a few punches, then back away. But he needn't have worried.

In the second round Fitzsimmons got in close and nailed Dunkhorst flush on the chin. The big man dropped like a sack of potatoes and failed to get up. Fitzsimmons had knocked out a man who weighed 140 pounds more than he did.

All for the Best

Sometimes success is due to a lucky break. Or what appears to be bad luck can really be a stroke of good fortune, although it doesn't seem that way at the time.

During World War I, Conn Smythe was a young officer with Canada's 40th Battery. He wasn't much of a hockey player, but he was an excellent judge of talent. Canada wanted men to enlist for service. Smythe was ordered to form a hockey team that would compete in the Senior Series of the Ontario Hockey Association.

Rival managers in the league knew Smythe was inexperienced. They also knew that very few fans attended hockey games right after Christmas. Therefore, they scheduled Smythe's first four games on his home ice at that time, figuring he wouldn't draw big crowds. Later the 40th Battery would play on the other teams' ice and they would collect the larger profits. Smythe didn't know the scheme. Innocently he agreed.

However, the 40th Battery did attract fans in their first three games. Then, just before the fourth game, the 40th received shipping orders. It would be their final game in Canada. They were going overseas.

Smythe decided to press his luck. The team's treasury had $7,000. He bet the whole amount on his team with some gamblers. In the locker room he told the players what he had done. They went out on the ice grimly and destroyed their opponents. Quinn Butterfield, one of the Battery's stars, scored five goals in the first eight minutes.

When Smythe came home, he tried for a job in big-league hockey. Colonel John S. Hammond, a wealthy New Yorker, bought a franchise that was called the Rangers. Smythe was commissioned to put together a team for Hammond.

The team Smythe assembled was loaded with future all-stars, including goalie Lorne Chabot; defensemen Ching Johnson and Taffy Abel; offensive specialists Frankie Boucher, Murray Murdoch, and the brothers Bill and Bun Cook. He got them all for $32,000. Experts said they were worth $250,000.

But someone convinced Hammond that Smythe wasn't experienced enough to manage a big-league team. Smythe was fired.

Still determined to get into hockey, Smythe began planning to buy the Toronto St. Patricks, which were for sale. But he didn't have enough money for the down payment. His main asset was a racehorse named Rare Jewel. Unfortunately Rare Jewel seemed to be a loser. Smythe raced the horse five times, and each time she finished last. Once, when Smythe bet that his horse *would* finish last, Rare Jewel finished next-to-last.

"What a nag," snorted Smythe. "Even when I pick her to finish last she can't do it."

Smythe got a new trainer named Dude Foden, who trained Rare Jewel properly. After a while Foden told Smythe the horse was ready to enter the Coronation Stakes race. Smythe took a chance and bet heavily. He bet win, place, and show (first, second, and third place).

Sure enough, Rare Jewel put on a burst of speed in the home stretch and won the race. For each $2 Smythe had bet to win, he received $219; for each place bet the payoff was $49; for the show bet it was $18. He bet his winnings on a couple of hockey games and won again. Then he bought the St. Patricks, changed the team's name to the Maple Leafs, and built the Maple Leaf Gardens.

Conn Smythe's "bad luck" was really good luck. If John Hammond had not fired him, he would probably not have tried to buy the St. Patricks. If Rare Jewel had not been such a loser in the beginning, the odds on the horse in the big race would not have been so high.

Upset

Man o' War was one of the greatest horses in the history of thoroughbred racing. In 1919–1920 the magnificent animal was entered in 21 races and won 20 of them.

The name of the horse that upset Man o' War was—*Upset.*

A LITTLE-KNOWN FIRST

In 1916 heavyweights Jess Willard and Frank Moran fought at Madison Square Garden in New York. There was nothing unusual about the fight itself, but it was the first time that women were permitted to attend a boxing bout in the United States.

Banned in Ireland

Hurling is a sport that originated in Ireland. Some sports historians say the game is almost 2,000 years old. The game is played mostly in Ireland or by small groups of Irish people living in other countries.

In hurling, a leather-covered ball (called a slitter) is caught on a stick with a wide curved blade (called a hurley). In order to score, the ball must be thrown into a net.

In 1884 the Gaelic Athletic Association established the rules for hurling. One of the rules stated that all hurling players and officials were prohibited from "playing, watching, or otherwise encouraging" the sports of soccer, rugby, or cricket. Those were games played by the hated British, and Ireland was then struggling to throw off British rule.

In 1922 Ireland gained its independence. But the rules forbidding any kind of association with rugby, soccer, or cricket are still in the book.

Baseball's Wackiest Inning

As a pitcher Al Schacht didn't last very long in big-league baseball. He pitched for the Washington Senators from 1919 to 1921, and his record was 14 won, 10 lost. However, Schacht was one of the zaniest men in any sport. Long after his active career was over, he continued to entertain fans as a baseball clown. Schacht enjoyed performing as much as the fans liked watching him.

After leaving the Senators, Schacht pitched for a while in the minor leagues, but he continued to amuse the customers. One of his routines involved a light fungo bat and a 10-cent baseball. He played "baseball-golf" with the bat and ball, driving it off a tee, then "putting" toward an imaginary hole.

Schacht did his fungo-baseball act while playing with Reading, Pennsylvania, and after he had finished his routine

he went back to the dugout. The saw-dust-filled ball was still in his pocket.

Toward the late innings Schacht was told to go to the bullpen just in case the Baltimore team staged a rally. Sure enough, in the ninth inning Schacht was called in to pitch. He still had that cheap baseball in his pocket.

Unable to resist the opportunity for a little fun, Schacht called his catcher to the mound for a conference. While no one was looking, he switched the dime-store ball for the real baseball.

"I've still got that goofy ball," he whispered to the befuddled catcher. "I want you to throw it back to me as soon as you catch it. I don't want the umpire to see it."

Schacht pitched the sawdust baseball right over the plate. The batter tagged it on the nose and lifted a soft pop fly to the pitcher. When Schacht caught the ball, he saw that it had been knocked a little lopsided. He squeezed it back into shape and faced the next hitter.

The same thing happened. Another little pop-up went back to the mound and

Schacht gloved it easily. But now the ball looked like a battered lump. Somehow Schacht made it look round and faced the Baltimore pitcher, Rube Parnham, who was a pretty good hitter.

Parnham really belted Schacht's pitch. The ball popped up, fluttered, dipped, and sailed like a wounded sparrow. Parnham watched in disbelief as Schacht caught it for the third out.

"I want you to look at that ball," roared the angry Parnham to the umpire.

The umpire walked out to the mound and took the ball from Schacht's mitt.

"It's the trick ball," Schacht explained, "but I got the first two out with the real ball. I was only having some fun. Parnham's not a nice guy and I wanted to show him up."

The umpire had to agree. Parnham was always "popping off" at other players. Seeing the umpire hesitate, Schacht pressed his advantage.

"Let him bat again," Schacht coaxed. "I'll use the real baseball."

Parnham took another turn at the plate, but by then he was so upset he couldn't control his swing. On the first pitch he hit a pop fly back to the pitcher.

Did Clancy Really Score?

One of the National Hockey League's early immortals was a player named Francis Michael "King" Clancy. He broke in during the 1922–1923 season as a defenseman. Today his name is entered in hockey's Hall of Fame.

For much of his rookie season Clancy saw no action at all. Finally, in overtime against Hamilton, he was sent into the game.

After the face-off, Clancy got possession of the puck. He passed to a teammate, then skated down the ice into the fray. Clancy got the puck back and took a wild swipe at it. The goal judge, standing behind the net, signaled a score.

The goalie protested that the puck had really gone in through the side of the net and shouldn't count. The official stood firm. That was how it went into the record book.

King Clancy had scored a goal on his first shot as a major-league hockey player.

Quiet on the Course!

Golfers are among the most high-strung and skittish of all athletes. The slightest noise from the gallery while they are preparing to swing can cause them to lose concentration. Many a tournament has been lost because of a stray sound from the spectators.

In 1960 the U.S. Open was played at the Cherry Hills Country Club near Denver, Colorado. Near the end of the third round the leader was Mike Souchak. He was four strokes ahead of the field. He teed up on the eighteenth hole, confident he would get at least a par and maintain his advantage.

Souchak raised his driver and prepared to send one out of sight. Just as he reached the top of his backswing, the silence was broken by a camera clicking loudly. Souchak was startled. Instead of a smooth swing, he pushed the drive out of bounds. He lost two strokes of his lead.

Souchak might have lost the tournament anyway. On the final round, played after lunch, he carded a 75. Arnold Palmer shot a 65 to win.

But it wasn't an alibi when Souchak explained what had happened. His fellow golfers understood. Souchak said, "All afternoon I kept thinking about that camera clicking, about the two strokes I lost and what they could mean. I just couldn't concentrate anymore."

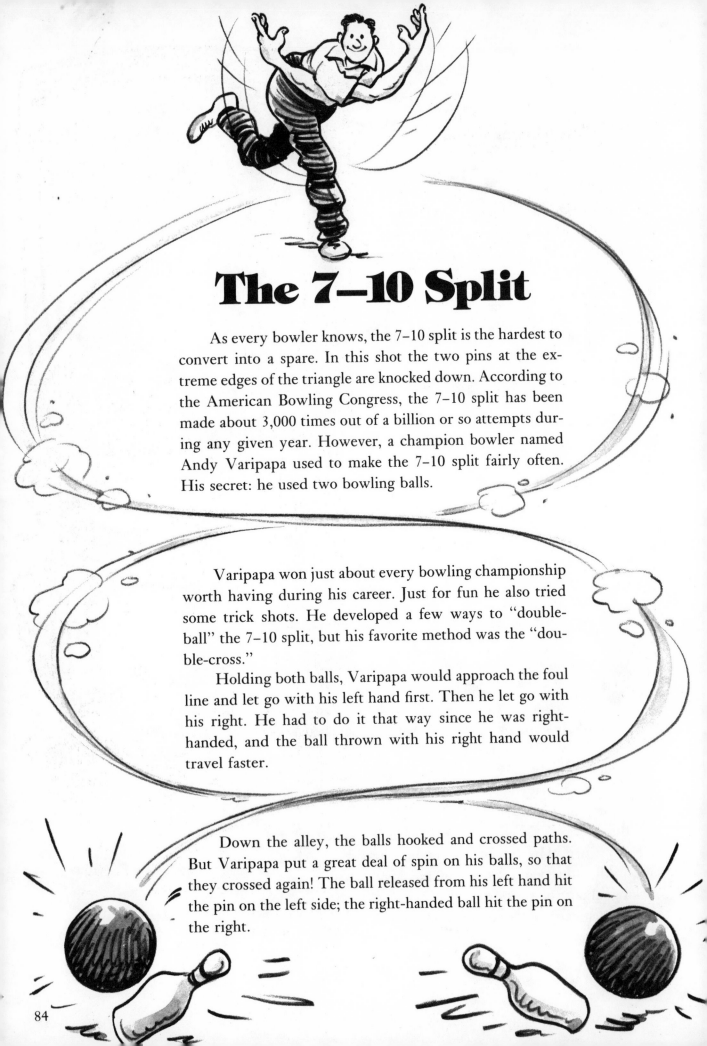

The 7–10 Split

As every bowler knows, the 7–10 split is the hardest to convert into a spare. In this shot the two pins at the extreme edges of the triangle are knocked down. According to the American Bowling Congress, the 7–10 split has been made about 3,000 times out of a billion or so attempts during any given year. However, a champion bowler named Andy Varipapa used to make the 7–10 split fairly often. His secret: he used two bowling balls.

Varipapa won just about every bowling championship worth having during his career. Just for fun he also tried some trick shots. He developed a few ways to "double-ball" the 7–10 split, but his favorite method was the "double-cross."

Holding both balls, Varipapa would approach the foul line and let go with his left hand first. Then he let go with his right. He had to do it that way since he was right-handed, and the ball thrown with his right hand would travel faster.

Down the alley, the balls hooked and crossed paths. But Varipapa put a great deal of spin on his balls, so that they crossed again! The ball released from his left hand hit the pin on the left side; the right-handed ball hit the pin on the right.

Heave-ho!

In Olympic weight lifting, there are three basic kinds of lifts: the military press, the snatch, and the clean-and-jerk.

In the military press, the lifter hoists the barbell to his shoulders or neck and holds it there for a few seconds. Then he raises the weights over his head.

The snatch is executed in one continuous movement. The lifter brings the barbell up high while the official counts 1 . . . 2.

The clean-and-jerk is like the military press, except that the lifter does not have to keep his toes on a line and is permitted to bend his knees during the lift.

Paul Anderson, an extraordinarily powerful man, weighed well over 300 pounds. He stood 5-foot-10. His wrist measured 9 inches around, his neck 23 inches. Anderson won the Olympic weight-lifting gold medal in 1956 in the heavyweight class. Shortly afterward he turned professional. On June 12, 1957, Anderson proved he was the strongest man in the world.

First, he had a table constructed that could stand up under tremendous weight. On top of the table was placed a steel safe. Just to add some additional pounds, a few heavy automobile parts were added. The total weight was 6,270 pounds.

Anderson knelt under the table. He placed his hands on a small stool for added support. Then he got his back under the table and lifted it a couple of inches off the ground.

To appreciate Anderson's feat, it should be noted that two old-fashioned, heavy, gas-guzzling station wagons would weigh about the same as the tonnage Anderson lifted.

THE GRAND OLD MAN OF FOOTBALL

His name was Amos Alonzo Stagg and he was born in 1862. Many football experts consider Stagg the most inventive coach in the history of football.

While still an undergraduate at Yale, Stagg invented the first tackling dummy. He merely hung a rolled-up mattress from the gymnasium ceiling, then placed another mattress underneath it. Later, as a coach, he devised the reverse play (Stagg called it "ends back"), the man-in-motion, the direct pass from center, and other plays.

Stagg was the Knute Rockne of his day, because he instilled fighting spirit in his teams.

Stagg first began to coach football at Springfield (Massachusetts) College. Another faculty member then was James Naismith, who invented basketball. In 1890 Stagg became the football coach at the new University of Chicago. He remained there for 41 years. His teams won 254, lost 104, and tied 28.

At the age of 70, Stagg had to quit coaching because of Chicago's retirement rule. He could have remained as an adviser at full salary, but Stagg liked to work with young people. He became head coach at the College of the Pacific for 14 years. Part of the time he had very few good players, because most of the young men were serving in the armed forces during World War II. Yet his Pacific teams won 59, lost 77, and tied 7.

Then the College of the Pacific asked him to retire because of his age. Again Stagg was offered an advisory job, but once more he refused. Stagg took a job at Susquehanna College, Pennsylvania, where his son, Alonzo, was head coach. The elder Stagg coached the offense. In 1951, Susquehanna enjoyed an undefeated season.

After that Stagg became the special kicking coach at Stockton Junior College in California. And finally, in 1960, he had to retire. By then he was 98 years old. He died in 1965 at the age of 102.

Strangely enough, Amos Alonzo Stagg did not set out to become a football coach. He entered Yale hoping to become a minister. He liked athletics well enough—in fact he was offered a lot of money to pitch for New York of the National League. As a football player, he was named to Walter Camp's All-American team. And Stagg was a very poor speaker. He soon realized that he would have great difficulty delivering a sermon before an audience.

The church lost a good minister, but football gained an immortal coach.

The Price Was Right

The fans of the Minneapolis Lakers seemed to lose interest in the basketball team after their great star George Mikan retired. By 1958 Bob Short, who owned the Lakers, was running out of cash. Short offered the team for sale to anyone who would pay him $250,000. There were no buyers, which turned out to be a lucky break for Mr. Short.

Short transferred the team to Los Angeles, and there the Lakers became an instant success. In 1964 he sold the basketball team to a Canadian millionaire named Jack Kent Cooke. The price was $5,175,000.

The Lady Is a Champ

Great Olympic athletes are measured by the number of medals they have won. In that case, the greatest of all Olympic athletes was a woman!

Larisa Latynina, a young Russian gymnast, won a total of six medals in 1956. Four were gold medals: for individual combined, team combined, horse vault, and floor exercises. She took a silver medal in the parallel bars and a bronze medal in the team (portable apparatus).

In 1960 Larisa won another six medals. Three were gold medals: for individual combined, team combined, and floor exercises. She won two silvers, for balance beam and parallel bars, plus one bronze in the horse vault.

In 1964 Larisa was again one of the stars of the Olympics, winning six more medals. She got two golds for team combined and floor exercises, two silvers for individual combined and horse vault, and two bronzes for balance beam and parallel bars.

Larisa Latynina won a total of 18 medals in Olympic competition. It is very difficult to imagine that *any* athlete will ever reach that total again.

Rainout

In January 1980 the State Fair Arena in Oklahoma suddenly began to spring a series of leaks. That was where Oklahoma City University played its home basketball games. A scheduled game against the University of Nevada at Las Vegas had to be postponed. That was probably college basketball's only rained-out game.

The Trade

It is not necessary to list all the baseball players involved in a trade at the time the swap is made. A player can be sent to another team in exchange for "a player to be named later." It happens quite often.

Years ago the New York Mets acquired a catcher named Harry Chiti from the Detroit Tigers, promising a player to be named later. However, after a time the Mets sent Chiti back to the Tigers. So it can be said that Harry Chiti was actually traded for himself!

THE OLD MAN STANDS IN

The finalists playing for the Stanley Cup in the 1927–1928 hockey season were the New York Rangers and the Montreal Maroons. The Rangers were coached by silver-haired Lester Patrick, one of the great names in hockey history.

The second game of that series provided one of hockey's greatest thrills. With four minutes of the first period gone, Nels Stewart of the Maroons grabbed the puck and fired a shot on goal. In those days masks for goalies were still unknown. The puck hit goalie Lorne Chabot over the eye. He fell to the ice unconscious.

The Rangers did not have a substitute goalie. However, a couple of goalies were in the stands as spectators. One was Alex Connell of the Ottawa Senators. He was one of the best in the National Hockey League. The other was Hugh McCormick, who played in the Canadian Pro League. Patrick went to Montreal manager Eddie Gerard and asked permission to use one of them in Chabot's place.

Gerard realized he had a chance to take the Stanley Cup because the Rangers had no backup goalie. He refused permission. In desperation, Patrick put on Chabot's gear himself.

It was a gamble. Patrick was 44 years old and had not played hockey for years. Once before he had tried his hand at goaltending with fair results. Now there was no one else he could call on to defend the net. There were still 16 minutes left in the first period, plus all of the second and third periods.

The rest of the Rangers did their best to defend coach Patrick. When the Maroons did get close enough for a shot, somehow Patrick managed to block it. It was a 0–0 tie, until New York's Bill Cook scored to make it 1–0.

Patrick couldn't shut out the Maroons forever. With six minutes left to play, Nels Stewart pounced on a rebound and slammed it into the net to tie the score. The game went into overtime.

Coach Patrick ached all over, but the cheering fans made him feel a little better somehow. At the seven-minute mark of overtime, Frankie Boucher split the Maroon defense, faked out the Maroon goalie, and scored the winning marker.

It had been an unbelievable performance by the old man. While Patrick was on the ice, the Maroons had taken 18 shots on goal and he had blocked 17 of them.

Rags to Riches

He began as a skinny young quarterback at St. Justin High School in Pittsburgh. Although he was good enough to be chosen for the all-Catholic team, no college seemed interested in giving him a football scholarship. And he could never afford to pay his own way through college. His mother delivered coal in the winter and scrubbed office floors during the summer. His father was dead.

Then the young man was invited to try out at the University of Louisville. The coach liked what he saw and awarded him a scholarship. The kid was pretty good, but certainly no college star.

In the college draft 200 players were picked ahead of him before the Pittsburgh Steelers called his name. But Pitt already had three quarterbacks and he was cut. At that point only the Cleveland Browns showed any interest, and they told him to try out the following year.

The young man never gave up on himself. To keep in shape he played sandlot football with the Bloomfield Rams for six dollars a game. He was noticed by Don Kellett, an executive with the Baltimore Colts, who saw him play and signed him with the team. But the rookie sat on the bench for the first four games. When the first-string quarterback was hurt, coach Weeb Ewbank sent the sub into action.

The youngster nobody wanted went on to become one of the greatest passers in the history of football. When he retired in 1973, he held numerous records, and was later inducted into the Hall of Fame.

His name? Why, Johnny Unitas—Mr. Quarterback!

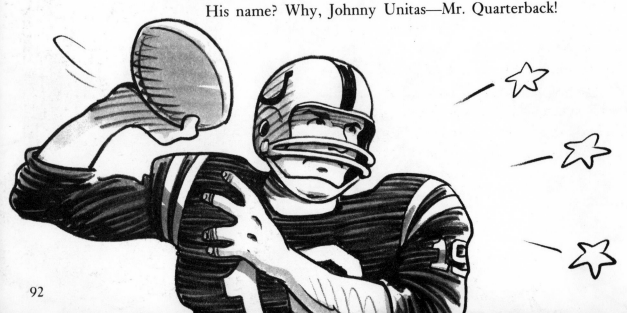

Cross-country Golf

Some golf courses are longer than others, but the one chosen by Floyd Satterlee Rood boggled the mind. His course was the *entire United States of America!*

On September 14, 1963, Rood took his first shot from a point just east of the Pacific Ocean surf. His game ended a little bit west of the Atlantic Ocean surf, on October 3, 1964. Thus Rood's course was 3,397.7 miles long.

For the record, he made it in 114,737 strokes, and he lost 3,511 golf balls.

The Fosbury Flop

Over the years athletic techniques have changed greatly. The way the high jump is executed today is the most dramatic example.

Using the old way of high jumping, the jumper ran up to the crossbar and leaped up on his inside foot. The side of his body was facing the bar. The jumper would roll his body over the bar face down and parallel to it, then land on his hands and knees in the sawdust.

By the time the 1968 Olympics arrived, the sawdust had been replaced by an air bag. Landing after a jump was a great deal softer and easier. An American high jumper named Dick Fosbury took advantage of the inflated bag to introduce a new method of high jumping.

After Fosbury took his running start toward the bar, he leaped up on his outside foot. He turned his back to the bar and went over it headfirst, landing on his shoulder blades. Had he landed on sawdust, he might have suffered a severe injury, but the inflated air bag cushioned his fall just fine.

Fosbury leaped 7 feet, 4½ inches, breaking the Olympic record. Today all high jumpers use the Fosbury Flop.

Ageless Aces

There is an old saying in sports, "Records are made to be broken." Golf is certainly no exception.

At one time Tommy Moore of Hagerstown, Maryland, was the youngest golfer ever to score a hole-in-one. Tommy was six years old when he got his ace in 1968 on the 145-yard fourth hole at Woodbrier Golf Course in Martinsburg, West Virginia.

Since then his record was broken by Coby Orr of Littleton, Colorado, in 1975. When he got his ace on the 103-yard fifth hole at Riverside Golf Course in San Antonio, Texas, Coby was five years old.

The oldest gentlemen ever to score holes-in-one were George Miller and Clark Youngman. Both were 93 years old. Miller got his ace on the 116-yard eleventh hole at the Anaheim Golf Course in California in 1970. Youngman scored his in 1971 at the Tam O'Shanter Club in Toronto.

Art Wall, Jr., holds the distinction of scoring the most holes-in-one. During the course of his career this marvelous professional golfer scored a total of 41 aces!

WHERE'S THAT DRAFT COMING FROM?

The Philadelphia Flyers came into the National Hockey League for the 1967–1968 season. The team proved to be very popular and drew good crowds, especially at home. Yet the Flyers had to play their last seven home games in Quebec, New York, and Toronto.

Why? Because the Spectrum, their home rink, seemed to be falling to pieces. Four times during the month of March 1968 the roof of the arena had been blown off.

Nice Toss, Joe

The Port Royal Golf Course in Bermuda is more than 6,000 yards long. On March 27, 1975, a young man named Joe Flynn scored an 82 over the 18 holes.

Flynn didn't use any golf clubs. He threw the ball.

Like Father, Like Son

Ted Williams of the Boston Red Sox was one of the greatest hitters ever to swing a baseball bat. During the course of his career he hit a total of 521 home runs. He played in the major leagues from 1939 until 1960, with time out for service in World War II and the Korean War.

During his early years Williams often faced a fine left-handed pitcher named Thornton Lee, who hurled for the Chicago White Sox. Williams hit several home runs off the deliveries of Thornton Lee.

By the time Williams was ready to retire in 1960, a young pitcher named Don Lee, Thornton's son, had come to the major leagues. Don Lee pitched for the Washington Senators.

On September 2, 1960, Ted Williams hit a home run off Don Lee. It was perhaps the only time in major league history that the same man hit home runs off both father and son.

Basketball's Greatest Team

In 1916 a team called the Original Celtics was formed. The players were part of an amateur community club in New York City at first, but two years later they turned professional. The team was managed by James and Thomas Furey, two sports promoters. The Celtics usually drew good crowds wherever they played.

The Celtics went on to become basketball's most famous team. In 1921–1922 they won the Eastern League championship, and the next year they won 13 straight. Then they quit the Eastern League to go on tour. They played 205 exhibition games and lost only 11.

Year after year the Celtics remained the top team in the United States. Sometimes the opposition was inferior, and the Celtics tried to add excitement to the games. The players would take it easy, making errors, letting the other team build up a lead. Then they would come from behind and just manage to pull the game out.

Sometimes their strategy backfired. Once they played a game against a pickup team, which was headed by Lou Gehrig, the first baseman of the New York Yankees. The Celtics probably forgot about the score. When they tried to rally, it was too late.

In 1926 the Celtics became part of the new American Basketball League. They represented Brooklyn, New York. Of course they won the championship. The next season the Celtics were switched to Manhattan, and a team called the Visitations took over the Brooklyn franchise. It made no difference; the Celtics won.

As the years passed, the magic of the Celtics began to fade. Different players and different owners seemed to change everything. At one time the team was owned by Kate Smith, the singing star. Finally, in 1941, the Celtics played a short exhibition game and disbanded forever.

It is practically impossible for any team to beat the records set by the Original Celtics. They racked up a total of 1,320 victories against only 66 defeats. Many of the players from the various rosters are in the Basketball Hall of Fame: Nat Holman, Joe Lapchick, Johnny Beckman, Henry "Dutch" Dehnert (he developed the pivot play), Stretch Meehan, Elmer Ripley, and many others. In the Naismith Hall of Fame there are numerous great stars enshrined, but only two complete teams. One is the team from Springfield, Massachusetts, that played basketball's first game in 1891. The other team is the immortal Original Celtics.

Dark Victory

In the ancient Olympics one of the roughest sports of all was a combination of boxing and wrestling called pancratium. There were no holds barred; everything was legal.

For example, the combatants wrapped metal-studded strips of leather around their fists. Choke holds were used. There were no weight classifications, so the larger man usually defeated the smaller man. There was no time limit. The bout went on until one man surrendered.

One of the champions of that era (about 700 B.C.) was a fighter named Arrachion. He won many such bouts—until he had to face a very formidable opponent. Arrachion had a twist hold on his opponent's foot, but his adversary grabbed Arrachion by the throat. With one supreme effort Arrachion wrenched his opponent's leg, causing the man to admit defeat. He lifted his arm to signal that he was finished.

As he did so, Arrachion choked to death. Yet Arrachion was declared the victor because his opponent gave in first.

SPORTS FIRST, SPOUSES LATER

The girls of the Kaizuka Amazons, a Japanese volleyball team, had no time for boyfriends. They got up early because they had to be at work in a factory by 8:00 A.M. They worked until 3:30, and by 4 in the afternoon they were practicing hard in an unheated gymnasium. Practice was over at midnight, and then the girls went home to get some rest so they could do the same thing the following day. Sunday was no holiday for the Amazons, because they practiced all day.

Often they were injured as they dived for the ball, skidded on the floor, or jammed their fingers against the ball. There were no extra benefits for their sacrifices, and their average salary was $50 a month. But they were dedicated to the sport.

For four years, starting in 1960, they were a winning team. They scored more than 100 straight victories. In 1963 the team won a world championship. Until that time, women's teams from Eastern Europe had usually won that title.

In 1964 the Amazons entered the Olympics, and that was when all their hard work paid off. They went into the finals against the Soviet Union and beat them in three sets. The Amazons were Olympic champions.

In Japan the girls became heroines. When the emperor heard they had been training for years and had had no time to meet boys, he asked the whole country to help find them husbands. After that the men came flocking.

The Pitchers' Series

There is a saying in baseball that pitching will dominate hitting in a World Series. Undoubtedly that sports proverb was born in 1905 when the New York Giants met the Philadelphia Athletics in the great autumn classic.

In the first game Christy Mathewson of the Giants defeated Philadelphia's Eddie Plank, 3–0.

In the second game Chief Bender of the Athletics bested Iron Man McGinnity of the Giants, 1–0.

In the third game Mathewson beat Andy Coakley of the A's, 9–0.

In the fourth game Plank and McGinnity hooked up in a pitching duel, which the Giants won, 1–0.

In the fifth game the magnificent Christy Mathewson defeated Chief Bender, 2–0.

It had truly been a pitchers' series. *Every game had been a shutout!*

The High Five

When athletes congratulate each other, they give the "high five." A player raises his arm high and his teammates take turns slapping his palm or clasping his hand.

It is believed that the inventor of this novel handshake was Derek Smith. He made it popular in the 1979–1980 season while playing on the University of Louisville basketball team, which won the national collegiate basketball title.

Look, But Don't Touch

There is only one sport in which none of the contestants has a chance of reaching the prize. That is greyhound racing. The dogs are not permitted to catch the mechanical rabbit.

Never Say Die

In the 1956 Olympics the United States was represented by the Yale rowing crew. Yale had a very strong group, and most experts thought it had a good chance to win. But in the first race Yale finished third behind Canada and Australia.

In many Olympic events one loss means elimination. But in rowing there is a kind of double elimination called repêchage (reh-peh-SHAHZH). A losing team can continue competing until it loses for the second time.

In the second race Yale defeated crews from Italy, Great Britain, and France. In the next race the Americans were pitted against Russia, Japan, and Australia. Once before, in the first race, Australia had defeated the American crew. Now Yale came out ahead, with Australia second.

Finally the Americans were matched against Canada and Australia. Both teams had beaten Yale once. This was the showdown race.

At first Canada led the way, but Australia caught up and passed them. Yale was rowing at the rate of 36 strokes a minute, which was faster than usual for them, but they kept up the pace. Soon they were dead even with the Canadians and Australians. Sensing victory, Yale increased the beat to 40 strokes per minute. Slowly they edged ahead. America won by a mere half-length. Australia was second, Canada third.

It had been a thrilling, come-from-behind victory. Yale captain Tom Charlton praised his own teammates and their opponents in the true spirit of Olympic competition. He said, "We're the toughest crews ever put together. And we beat the best."

SHUTOUT GOALIE

On February 24, 1949, Roy Conacher of the Chicago Black Hawks scored against goalie Bill Durnan of the Montreal Canadiens. There were still 43 minutes and 45 seconds left to play in the hockey game. Durnan allowed no further scoring.

Two days later Durnan had a shutout against the Detroit Red Wings. In the next game Durnan blanked the Toronto Maple Leafs. After that he shut out the Boston Bruins. In the following game he shut out Boston again.

Finally the Canadiens played the Black Hawks again. At the six-minute mark Gaye Stewart finally got the puck past Durnan and scored.

Oddly, it was after a goal by a Black Hawk player that the shutout streak began, and a goal by another Black Hawk that it ended. In between, Durnan logged 309 minutes and 21 seconds of scoreless play—more than five hours of shutout hockey!

Long-Distance Throw

Much has been written about the "tape measure" home runs hit by such baseball sluggers as Mickey Mantle and Babe Ruth. But how far can anyone throw a baseball?

That question was answered in Cincinnati on October 12, 1910. An outfielder named Sheldon LeJeune threw a baseball 426 feet, 9½ inches. It remains the longest baseball throw ever measured.

Grand Slam

Over the years there have been many great golfers: Ben Hogan, Arnold Palmer, Jack Nicklaus, and others. But none of them ever matched the achievement of Bobby Jones in 1930. That was the year Jones won the Grand Slam of golf.

First he won the British Amateur title at St. Andrews, Scotland. After that came victory in the British Open. It was followed by a win in the U.S. Open and, finally, the U.S. Amateur.

Jones retired from competition at the age of 28. He never turned professional.

Triple Champ

In modern boxing, when the champion in a division wins the title in a higher weight classification, he must give up the crown he has won at the lower weight. For example, if the bantamweight champion (118-pound limit) defeats the featherweight champion (126-pound limit), he must give up his bantamweight title.

Before this rule was instituted, a boxer named Henry Armstrong was permitted to hold the three championships he had won. From August to December 1938 Armstrong was the recognized champion of the featherweight, lightweight, and welterweight divisions.

Statistics

How many runs have been scored so far in baseball's major leagues? At one time that question might have seemed foolish, but in this computer age it is possible to figure out almost any puzzle.

On May 4, 1975, when big-league baseball was in its ninety-ninth year, Bob Watson of the Houston Astros scored what appeared to be merely another run. However, according to some statisticians, that was the one-millionth run scored in the big leagues.

The Seiko Time Corporation has projected that run number 2,000,000 will be scored in June 2042.

HOW TWO-PLATOON FOOTBALL BEGAN

Before 1945 nearly every football player had to play both offense and defense. All the pros were 60-minute men. They would leave the game only if injured or to take a brief rest. Even the quarterback, often the lightest player on the team, had to make tackles.

During World War II most of America's young men were in the armed services. Military teams, such as Great Lakes Naval Training Station, had outstanding teams. The best team in college football was Army, which had the cream of the crop. Fullback "Doc" Blanchard tore holes in the line and was nicknamed Mr. Inside. Halfback Glenn Davis, the fast ball carrier who went around end, was Mr. Outside.

By September 1945 the war was over but very few servicemen were back in school yet. Most college players were very young and had little experience. A

team of such players was Fritz Crisler's University of Michigan squad. Army was on Michigan's schedule, and Crisler knew his boys had little chance to beat the Cadets. But as he watched the Michigan team practice, he noticed that some players were better on defense, others on offense.

Crisler divided his team into units. When Michigan had the ball, their offensive unit played. When their opponents had possession, the Michigan defensive unit went in. Football fans were treated to the unusual sight of an entire team leaving the field, to be replaced by another entire team.

In the Army game Crisler's plan worked well for three periods. But nobody could hold Army forever. The Cadets won, 28–7. But Crisler's tactics had held the score down.

Officials were puzzled by the unlimited substitution at first. They tinkered with the rules. They decided that if a player was taken out of the game in one quarter, he couldn't return until the next period. But that change didn't work out well. As the years passed, new methods of attack and defense were developed until Fritz Crisler's two-platoon football eventually became firmly established.

60-minute men

HUFF! PUFF!

GASP!

Set 'Em Up, Doc

Ivan "Ching" Johnson was an outstanding defenseman with the New York Rangers during the 1920s. He was a rugged hockey player, totally unafraid, and would bang into any opponent without blinking. To be sure, he was injured quite often. There were few bones in his body that were not broken at one time or another.

There was one oddity about Johnson—he didn't drink alcohol. Nearly every other hockey player of that era was known to take a nip now and then, but not Johnson.

Once he got into a slam-bang brawl and was shaken up. He went to the dressing room, where the doctor looked him over.

"You're all right, Ching," said the doctor. "What you need is a glass of whiskey to make you relax."

"Whatever you say," mumbled the weary Johnson.

Ching gulped the bourbon and went back on the ice. He became rubber-legged and zigzagged around the rink while the fans watched with amusement and amazement. Then Johnson got possession of the puck. He wobbled in on the goalie, shot—and scored!

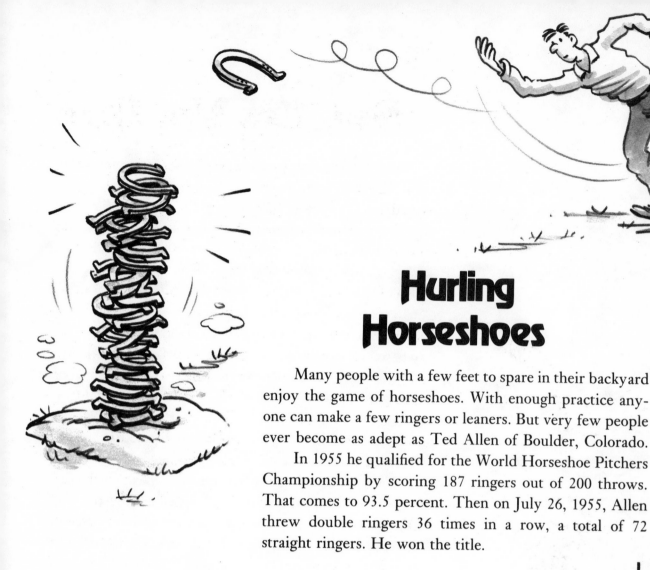

Hurling Horseshoes

Many people with a few feet to spare in their backyard enjoy the game of horseshoes. With enough practice anyone can make a few ringers or leaners. But very few people ever become as adept as Ted Allen of Boulder, Colorado.

In 1955 he qualified for the World Horseshoe Pitchers Championship by scoring 187 ringers out of 200 throws. That comes to 93.5 percent. Then on July 26, 1955, Allen threw double ringers 36 times in a row, a total of 72 straight ringers. He won the title.

The Singing Swinger

Jimmy Demaret was one of the best golfers of his era. He was the first to win the Masters Tournament three times. Demaret was also a very good singer. Every once in a while he would sing with Ben Bernie's orchestra. Bernie was a very popular bandleader and had his own radio program. Demaret was so well liked that he gave up golf temporarily. In 1935, when he wasn't doing too well on the golf course, Demaret sang with Bernie's band full-time.

The .400 Hitter

It is the dream of every major-league hitter that someday he will bat .400. As a rookie in 1939 Ted Williams batted .327, and the following year he hit .344. In 1941 he began to terrorize opposing pitchers in earnest. By midseason he was batting .405.

In order to hit .400 a batter must get two base hits in every five at-bats. Only seven major leaguers had reached that mark: Ty Cobb, Rogers Hornsby, Napoleon Lajoie, Harry Heilmann, George Sisler, "Shoeless" Joe Jackson, and Bill Terry. Many players had batted .390 or more, but .400 was the charmed circle.

Through August and September, Williams kept up his blistering pace, but by the final week of the season he was at .399. Red Sox manager Joe Cronin offered to give Ted a rest so that he would be fresh for the last couple of games.

"No," Williams said quietly. "Either I can hit .400 for a whole season or I can't. I'm going to find out."

The last day of the season the Red Sox played the Philadelphia Athletics. In his first at-bat Ted got a single. The next time up he socked a home run. Then he got two more hits. In his fifth trip to the plate he was robbed of yet another hit. But he had 4 for 5, more than enough to boost him over the .400 mark.

That day the Sox were playing a doubleheader. No doubt other players than Williams might have been content to sit on the bench to preserve the .400 average. Ted insisted on playing. He got two hits in three at-bats. His final average was .406.

ON THE FIRING LINE

On the average during the course of a hockey season, a team may have between 30 and 40 shots on goal. Sometimes they shoot more, sometimes less.

On March 4, 1941, goalie Sam LoPresti of the Chicago Black Hawks must have thought the Boston Bruins had declared war on him. In that game Boston took 83 shots on goal—a record. LoPresti blocked all but three. The Black Hawks lost by a score of only 3–2.

Old Hoss Radbourn

Back in the 1870s and 1880s baseball rules were quite different from what they are today. For instance, a pitch could be delivered to the plate on one bounce. If it crossed the plate after bouncing, it could still be called a strike. Pitchers stood 50 feet from the plate instead of the modern 60 feet, 6 inches. It took seven balls to walk a batter, and some pitchers even threw underhand. In the early 1880s, if a batter hit a foul and it was caught on the first bounce, he was out.

But regardless of the rules, one pitcher of that era stood head and shoulders above the rest. His name was Charles G. Radbourn, but everyone called him Old Hoss. His achievements during the 1884 season were spectacular.

On August 7 that year, playing for Providence, Rhode Island, Radbourn pitched against New York and won, 4–2. Two days later he pitched against Boston and won, 1–0, in 11 innings. After resting a day, Old Hoss beat Boston again, 3–1. The very next day Radbourn beat Boston again, 4–0.

Radbourn wanted to take a day off after that, but a friend came to him and begged him to pitch again. He had bet $6,000 on the game coming up.

"Guess I might as well," Radbourn sighed. "I pitched 'em all so far, might as well do the job right."

Old Hoss did pitch, and he beat Boston, 1–0.

The record book shows that Old Hoss Radbourn won 60 games and lost only 12 in 1884. He pitched a total of 678 ⅔ innings, striking out 441 batters.

It is fairly safe to say that no other pitcher will even approach that record.

No Score from the Floor

The second game of the 1953 NBA finals between the New York Knicks and the Minneapolis Lakers produced some of the strangest basketball ever seen. During the final nine minutes of the game, neither side could score a basket from the floor!

Both teams did manage to score a few foul shots, but although they took numerous shots from the floor, none went through the hoop. Nothing like that had ever happened in a playoff game before, and nothing like that has happened since.

Stepchildren

In 1932 the Colgate football team was undefeated, untied, and unscored-upon. But they did not receive an invitation to the Rose Bowl, although they were considered the top college team in the country.

Private Enterprise

Mark Warrilow was an enterprising Englishman. In a suburb of London he built a new swimming pool, 100 by 120 feet, and filled it with half a million gallons of water. Then he opened for business.

Almost nobody came. It was a cold summer and the pool was not heated. Warrilow was faced with financial disaster. But he got a brilliant idea and soon was happily counting the gate receipts.

He dumped truckloads of sand and gravel into the pool, completely covering the bottom. Then he stocked the pool with sleek trout. Sure enough, the crowds came, but they weren't swimmers, they were fishermen.

WHAT'S IN A NAME?

On September 16, 1934, John Baylor of Washington, D.C., was told he had just become the father of a baby boy. Mr. Baylor glanced at his watch to note the time he heard the news. His watch was an Elgin. And that was how Elgin Baylor, one of basketball's greatest stars, got his name.

Where's That Cup?

Many a National Hockey League player who has won a major award—Rookie of the Year, Most Valuable Player, and so on—has stated that he would willingly trade his personal honors if his team could win the Stanley Cup. In pro hockey it is almost a religious object. Yet this great symbol has been abused on occasion. Once a member of the winning Ottawa team kicked the Cup into the Rideau Canal, but the canal was frozen and the Cup was recovered. Another time someone connected with the Kenora Thistles Hockey Club got angry and threatened to throw it into a lake.

The zaniest Stanley Cup adventure happened one year when Montreal won it. Some players began to celebrate. After a few drinks they began to drive around in an automobile with the Cup. The car had a flat and the players got out to change the tire. The Cup was placed on the sidewalk. When the flat was fixed, the players drove away and left the Cup where they had put it. No doubt, had the trophy been lost, the fans and team officials would have slaughtered the inebriated players. Fortunately someone in the car missed the Cup. The car was turned around and the men went looking for it.

The symbol of hockey's championship was still there on the sidewalk.

Strikeout Artist

Ron Necciai (NETCH-eye) was 19 years old when he reported to Bristol of the Class D Appalachian Baseball League. He was a right-handed pitcher just out of high school. On May 13, 1952, he faced the Welch, West Virginia, team in a regular league game.

Necciai struck out the first four men he faced. Then a batter sent a routine grounder to shortstop and was thrown out. Necciai struck out the following batter.

Then Necciai began to strike out the batters as fast as they stepped up to the plate. One batter walked and another was hit by one of Necciai's pitches, but everybody else returned forlornly to the bench.

In the top of the ninth Necciai fanned the first two batters. Now he had 25 strikeouts. Necciai got three strikes on the next batter, but his catcher, Harry Dunlop, dropped the third strike and the batter scampered to first. According to baseball rules, in such situations the catcher is given an error and the pitcher is credited with a strikeout. Necciai refused to be ruffled. He struck out the next batter to finish the game.

Not only did Ron Necciai pitch a no-hitter, but he struck out 27 batters! Only one batter, in the second inning, managed to hit the ball fairly and he was thrown out.

Necciai continued his amazing pitching in his next two games. He struck out 20, then 19 batters. The Bristol team was the property of the Pittsburgh Pirates of the National League. It was a big jump from Class D to the major leagues but the Pirates decided to see what Necciai could do.

Necciai was not very effective. He did strike out 31 batters, but won only one of seven decisions. He suffered a sore arm and ulcers and went back to the minors for a short time. Then he left baseball for good.

Howdy, Pardners

In 1940 the Masters Golf Tournament was won by Jimmy Demaret. Lloyd Mangrum finished second, Byron Nelson was third, and Henry Cooper ended in fourth place.

All four golfers were from Texas.

Survivor

In the early days of competitive skiing, one of the greatest skiers was Mathias Zdarsky. He was the first person in Austria to teach skiing on a regular basis, and by 1904 he had about 1,000 students. Zdarsky is now considered by many to be the father of the Alpine technique. It was Zdarsky who introduced the snowplow to skiing. To execute the snowplow both skis are pointed inward. This enables the skier to slow down. Zdarsky also introduced the stem turn, in which the skier changes direction by pushing one heel out while moving fast.

But Mathias contributed more than skiing maneuvers to snow sports. Once he was caught in an avalanche and suffered more than 80 fractures. But he survived and later wrote a book about avalanches that proved to be very useful.

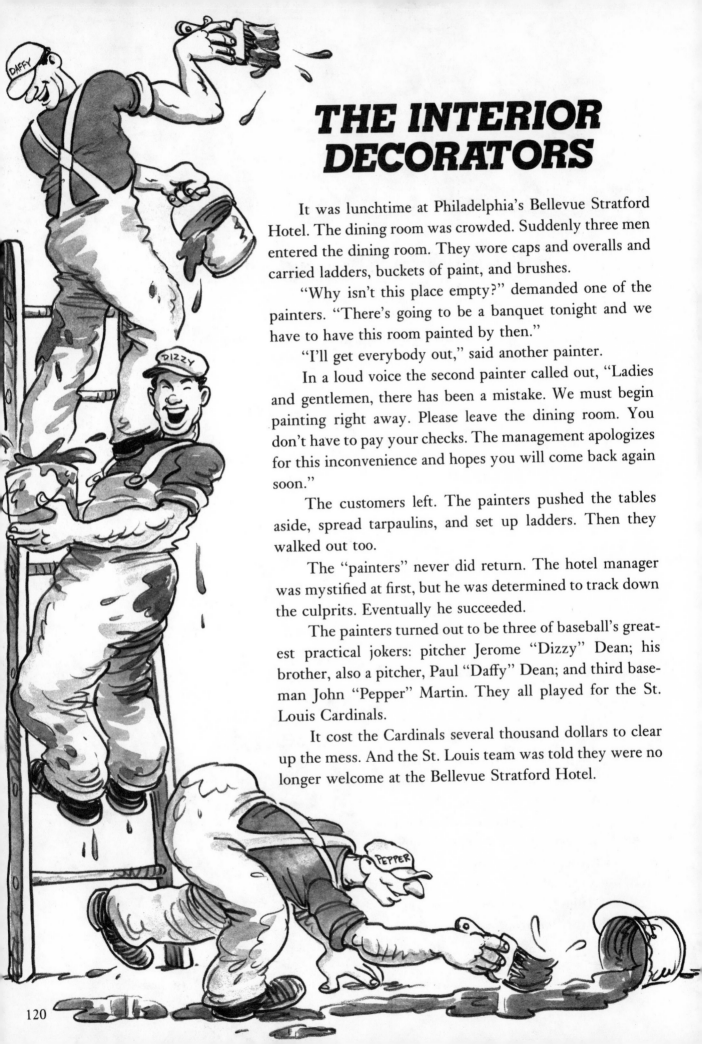

THE INTERIOR DECORATORS

It was lunchtime at Philadelphia's Bellevue Stratford Hotel. The dining room was crowded. Suddenly three men entered the dining room. They wore caps and overalls and carried ladders, buckets of paint, and brushes.

"Why isn't this place empty?" demanded one of the painters. "There's going to be a banquet tonight and we have to have this room painted by then."

"I'll get everybody out," said another painter.

In a loud voice the second painter called out, "Ladies and gentlemen, there has been a mistake. We must begin painting right away. Please leave the dining room. You don't have to pay your checks. The management apologizes for this inconvenience and hopes you will come back again soon."

The customers left. The painters pushed the tables aside, spread tarpaulins, and set up ladders. Then they walked out too.

The "painters" never did return. The hotel manager was mystified at first, but he was determined to track down the culprits. Eventually he succeeded.

The painters turned out to be three of baseball's greatest practical jokers: pitcher Jerome "Dizzy" Dean; his brother, also a pitcher, Paul "Daffy" Dean; and third baseman John "Pepper" Martin. They all played for the St. Louis Cardinals.

It cost the Cardinals several thousand dollars to clear up the mess. And the St. Louis team was told they were no longer welcome at the Bellevue Stratford Hotel.

Now That's Big!

Modern basketball players tend to be pretty tall, but no one has ever matched the height of Suleiman Ali Nashnush, who played for the Libyan National team in 1962. Ali was eight feet tall, making him the biggest basketball player on record.

Jaws

Movie fans who saw the picture *Jaws* realized that they were seeing a kind of mechanical monster. After all, a real white shark would probably fail to follow the script when the movie director set the cameras rolling.

On April 21, 1959, a fisherman named Alf Dean hooked a white shark near Ceduna, South Australia. This was no machine that followed its cues. The battle went on for a long time. When the great white shark was finally landed, it was measured. It weighed 2,664 pounds, was 16 feet, 10 inches long, and came to 9 feet, 6 inches in girth. It was the biggest fish ever landed by rod, reel, and hook.

Quick Winning Streak

Numerous teams have won five straight football games, but it usually takes five weeks to accomplish the feat. The University of the South—once known as Sewanee—did it in *six days!*

For a reason never fully explained, coach Luke Lea scheduled the games against some of the best teams in the region. All games were on the road.

On November 8, 1899, Sewanee met unbeaten Texas and defeated them, 12–0. The next day they beat Texas A & M, 32–0. After that they took on Tulane and won again, 23–0.

Now it was Sunday, a day of rest. The boys from Sewanee took a well-deserved break.

Back to the football wars went coach Lea's squad. Louisiana State fell, 34–0. Finally, to end matters, Mississippi State was conquered, 12–0.

Sewanee had faced some formidable opposition. A couple of their victims had been undefeated before knocking heads with the visitors. Yet *nobody had scored on Sewanee!*

The "march through the South" was all the more remarkable because Sewanee had taken only 12 players on the trip. But there weren't many more they could have recruited. The entire college had a total enrollment of only 97 male students.

I Paid, Didn't I?

In the early years of hockey one of the roughest players was a firebrand named Ken Randall. He was constantly being fined because of fights, and the fines totaled up. Randall didn't always pay on time, and finally he owed $35, a lot of money in those days.

League officials grew tired of Randall's tardy payments and ordered him to come across with the money or be suspended. Randall didn't like to be bullied, but he liked suspension even less. He got back at the officials by offering them $32 in bills, plus a roll of 300 pennies.

But the pennies were considered unacceptable. Randall carried on his joke by placing the roll of pennies on the ice. Someone poked the roll hard and the pennies went spilling all over the rink. That did it! The officials ordered the players to pick up all the pennies, and Randall had to pay the missing $3 in bills. He paid.

SOME FAMILY!

Mike Turnesa was a groundskeeper at the Fairview Country Club in Elmsford, New York. Mike Turnesa had seven sons: Mike, Jr.; Frank; Joe; Phil; Doug; Jim; and Willie. Papa Turnesa taught them how to play golf almost as soon as they were old enough to hold a club.

In time the first six Turnesa boys became professional golfers. Only Willie, the youngest, did not. But Willie was probably as good a golfer as his older brothers. He won the U.S. Amateur championship in 1938 and 1948, and the British Amateur title in 1947.

The other Turnesas won a lot of tournaments. In 1952 brother Jim won the Professional Golfers Association (PGA) title.

Sportsmanship

At the end of every basketball all-star game, a trophy is awarded to the Most Valuable Player. In 1959 the vote for MVP ended in a tie between veteran Bob Pettit and rookie Elgin Baylor. A tie had never happened before, and the officials obviously were not expecting one, because there was only one trophy to be awarded.

At this point Pettit walked over to Baylor and shook his hand. "You take it," he told the young star. "I've won the award before. I can wait for my duplicate."

Pettit knew how much it meant to Baylor to win the award in his first pro season, and how proud he would be to walk off the court with it.

Bobo Always Forgot to Duck

Norman Louis "Bobo" Newsom was a very good pitcher who won more than 200 games in his major-league career. He was somewhat zany and quite talkative. Bobo also had a very hard head.

While he was with the Washington Senators, Bobo pitched the opening game of the 1936 season against the New York Yankees. President Franklin Delano Roosevelt was watching the game.

In the third inning Ben Chapman, the speedy Yankee outfielder, dropped a bunt down the third-base line. Third baseman Ossie Bluege raced in, grabbed the ball with his bare hand, and fired it toward first base. Normally the pitcher drops to his knees in such a situation, in order to give the infielder a clear view of first base. For some reason Newsom didn't duck. The ball smacked against Newsom's jaw with great force.

Newsom's head jerked back. He reeled, staggered, and wobbled around the infield holding his head. Time-out was called while his teammates gathered around him.

"Are you okay, Bobo?" Bluege asked anxiously. "Should we get an ambulance?"

"Wow, what a sock," gasped Newsom. Then he said, "Hey, the President came to see ol' Bobo pitch, so I'll pitch."

Bobo hung in and pitched a 1–0 shutout over the Yanks.

On another occasion a batter belted a line drive right back at the pitcher's box. The ball hit Bobo just above the forehead and bounced into center field. Time-out was called. Bobo assured everyone he was all right, and he proceeded to finish the game. Between innings he told his teammates that he was "hearing pretty music."

That night a newly married sportswriter met Bobo in the lobby of a hotel and introduced him to his bride. Bobo bowed courteously and said, "Madam, would you like to feel the bump on my head?"

Sometimes Bobo talked too much, and that was the reason he had another close encounter with a baseball. In 1935 he faced Earl Averill of the Cleveland Indians. Averill was one of the hardest hitters in the American League. Bobo slipped over two quick strikes and then began to taunt the batter.

"Earl," he called out, "the next pitch is comin' in over the outside corner, waist high."

Bobo pitched and Averill swung. The ball came zooming off the bat and struck Bobo in the leg. He hobbled after the bounding sphere and managed to throw Averill out at first. However, Bobo's bragging was a costly mistake. Although he managed to finish the game, Averill's drive had broken a bone in Bobo's kneecap and the pitcher was sidelined for five weeks.

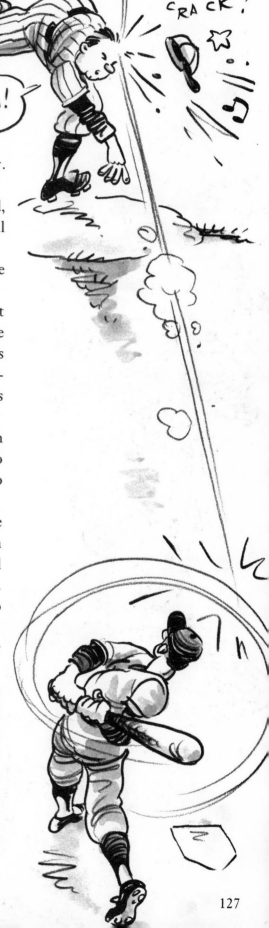

Too Good to Hide

Joe Medwick had been an outstanding all-around athlete at Carteret High School in New Jersey. He had hopes of getting an athletic scholarship to Notre Dame, but he never received an offer. However, Medwick was approached by Charlie Kelchner, a scout for the St. Louis Cardinals. Kelchner wanted to sign the teenager to a minor-league contract.

"Gee, I don't know," Medwick said doubtfully. "I'm still hoping for that Notre Dame scholarship."

"Why not use a different name?" Kelchner suggested.

Many students used false names and played ball during the summer months. Lou Gehrig was just one example. Kelchner thought up the name Mickey King.

"Use that name," Kelchner said. "Play baseball, and if the scholarship comes, go to college during the fall and winter. If you don't make good, who's going to know? Nobody notices a mediocre player."

Medwick agreed. But the scheme didn't work. Medwick played 75 games with a team in Scottsdale, Pennsylvania. He batted .419, got 139 hits, and drove in 100 runs. Before long everybody knew that Mickey King was really Joe Medwick.

Joe Medwick became one of baseball's best right-handed batters. In 1937 he won baseball's Triple Crown.

A Ball of a Different Color

For as long as anyone can remember, golf balls have been white. That is beginning to change. Many experts feel that before too long, the white ball will be a museum piece.

Golfers have often complained that it is difficult to follow the flight of a white golf ball as it soars through the air on a long drive. Often it gets lost against the white clouds in the sky. It can also be difficult to locate a white ball that lands in the rough.

A few professional golfers have already switched. They use orange or yellow balls, even in tournaments. Jack Nicklaus, who is color-blind where red and green are concerned, has asked one company to develop a fluorescent golf ball that will be a golden yellow.

ALL-AROUND ATHLETE

Many athletes in the various major leagues excel at more than one sport. For example, basketball star Dave DeBusschere of the Detroit Pistons and New York Knicks also played major-league baseball with the Chicago White Sox. Jackie Robinson was a college All-American football player in addition to becoming the major league's first black baseball player. No one, however, was as versatile as Lionel "Big Train" Conacher, who played in the National Hockey League for several years.

Lionel was an outstanding baseball player with the old Toronto Maple Leafs of the Triple-A International League. Ty Cobb once watched him play and said he could make it into the big leagues. In addition, Conacher was the Canadian light-heavyweight boxing champion and once sparred a couple of rounds with Jack Dempsey. Big Train also played pro football with the Toronto Argonauts. And he was a dandy lacrosse player.

As a young man Conacher was constantly busy with athletics. Once he played a baseball game and tripled home the winning run. Then he raced to the other side of town to play in a lacrosse match. When he arrived, the game was already in progress and his team was losing, 3–0. Conacher put on a uniform and joined the action. He scored four goals, got an assist for another, and his team won.

Because his family was too poor to buy skates, Big Train didn't learn to skate until he was sixteen years old. Only six years later he became a pro hockey player.

He Never Missed

From 1965 through 1968 Kim Braswell was the place-kicker at Avondale (Georgia) High School. During that time he attempted 134 points-after-touchdown. He made good on all 134. He also tried three field goals, from the 43-yard line, the 38-yard line, and the 33-yard line. He made good on all three attempts.

No Record

Is it possible for *anyone* to run a measured mile in 3 minutes, 31.25 seconds? It happened, but it can never be entered in the record book.

In April 1982 an American named Steve Scott ran the mile in the time indicated. In second place, with a time of 3 minutes, 32.25 seconds, was Mike Hillardt of Australia. The third spot went to Ray Flynn of Ireland at 3 minutes, 32.75 seconds. John Walker of New Zealand came in fourth at 3 minutes, 33.93 seconds.

However, the race was run downhill on the main street of Auckland, New Zealand. Races are always run on level ground. Over the mile distance the street dropped 200 feet.

Double Victory

Years ago in the minor leagues, one of baseball's strangest plays occurred, and it took the president of the league to force a decision on both teams.

Texarkana was playing against Sherman. In the bottom of the ninth Texarkana had a man on third with two out. The batter had two strikes on him.

As the pitcher wound up for his next delivery, the base runner tried to steal home. The pitch was taken at the plate. The runner slid home and the umpire called him safe.

It should have been the winning run, but the manager of the Sherman team came charging off the bench to confront the umpire.

"Was that last pitch a ball or a strike?" he demanded. "Listen, ump, if it was a strike, the batter is out on strikes and the run doesn't count. If it was a ball,

okay, the winning run has scored. Now, was it a ball or a strike?"

The umpire was dumbfounded. "I don't know," he admitted sheepishly. "I was busy watching the runner and I didn't pay attention to the pitch."

The other umpire was equally unsure. He too had been watching the runner.

The league president was present at the game, and although he as well had been watching the runner, he had to make a decision.

"The run doesn't count," he said.

The game had to be resumed the next day in the tenth inning. Sherman scored two runs, but a three-run homer gave the victory to Texarkana.

The Texarkana manager was still angry about the decision. "We had to win that game twice," he declared.

Record Breaker

Of all the Olympic athletes in history, Al Oerter of the United States was the most consistent. Nobody could beat him in the discus throw.

Oerter entered the 1956 Olympics and won the event with a record-breaking throw of 184 feet, 10 ½ inches. After that he won in the 1960, 1964, and 1968 Olympics. Each time he set a record, but the last three records he broke were his own.

WHERE IN THE HECK IS MAUCH CHUNK?

NEW TOWN

Jim Thorpe was considered America's greatest athlete during the first half of the twentieth century. Thorpe was a Sac and Fox Indian. He attended the Indian Training School at Carlisle, Pennsylvania. Thorpe died in 1953.

The following year the small communities of Lower Mauch Chunk, Upper Mauch Chunk, and East Mauch Chunk, Pennsylvania, decided to become a single town. They called it Jim Thorpe, Pennsylvania. The population then was 5,300.

The Birth of the Forward Pass

In the beginning football was a brutal game. From the middle 1880s and through much of the early 1900s, one of the most popular plays was the wedge. The team with the ball would form a kind of V (wedge). The ball carrier would be in the middle of the V. The formation would then slash through the defense. Players suffered bruises and broken bones in this kind of plan. Some were even killed.

In those days there was no such play as a forward pass. It was illegal. John Heisman, the coach at Auburn, saw a game that offered a possible solution to the roughness of football as it was then played.

In 1895, during a game between North Carolina and Georgia, the North Carolina fullback was trying to punt. Georgia came in fast and the kicker had to scramble. Just as he was about to be brought down, the harassed player threw the ball downfield. A North Carolina teammate saw the ball in the air and caught it. He ran for a touchdown.

The Georgia coach screamed to the referee about the touchdown. The referee said he didn't see the throw, all he saw was a North Carolina player running for a touchdown, although he didn't

know how that player had gotten the ball.

John Heisman thought about that play for a long time. He came to the conclusion that if more passes were thrown, fewer wedge plays would be run. But although he tried to influence various officials, at first nobody would listen to him. He made such a pest of himself that after a time the whole idea became known as "Heisman's forward pass."

Football became such a rough game that President Theodore Roosevelt threatened to abolish the sport if new rules were not made immediately. So in 1906 a form of forward passing was permitted.

In the beginning it didn't work well for several reasons. First, a pass had to cross the line of scrimmage not more than five yards on either side of the center. In other words, it could be thrown only into the middle of the field. Second, an incomplete pass could be recovered by the defensive team, just as if it had been a

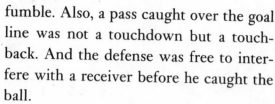

fumble. Also, a pass caught over the goal line was not a touchdown but a touchback. And the defense was free to interfere with a receiver before he caught the ball.

Most important of all, nobody really knew how to throw a forward pass. The passer would grip the ball any old way and just heave it over the line in a wobbly arc. But one smart coach figured out the correct way to throw a ball. His name was Eddie Cochems, the head man at St. Louis University. He discovered that the ball would spiral accurately when gripped with the fingers across the laces. He taught his passer, Brad Robinson, how to throw the ball. Robinson and teammate Jack Schneider formed the first great passer-receiver combination in football.

Still, very few colleges used the forward pass as a regular play. Not until 1913 did it become popular, as a result of a game between mighty Army and little known Notre Dame. Army expected no difficulty in beating the small college located in South Bend, Indiana. But the forward pass helped Notre Dame whip Army, 35–13.

The passer was Gus Dorais. The receiver went on to immortality as Notre Dame's coach. His name was Knute Rockne. After Dorais and Rockne showed what could be done with the forward pass, every team began to use it effectively.

So, because of an illegal play in 1895, the forward pass became the most important weapon in offensive football.

Too Much of a Good Thing

Any Stanley Cup game is charged with excitement, but no one was prepared for the action of the 1936 semifinal hockey game between the Detroit Red Wings and the Montreal Maroons. It began on March 24 and did not end until the following day.

After three periods of regulation-time hockey the score was tied at 0–0. The first overtime period saw no goals. Neither did the second, third, or fourth. Both teams almost scored in the fifth overtime period, but great defensive play prevented a goal.

The game finally ended after 16 minutes and 30 seconds of the sixth overtime period when Hec Kilrea of Detroit passed to teammate Moderre "Mud" Bruneteau, who poked the puck into the net.

By then it was 2:25 in the morning. The teams had played almost *nine* periods of hockey in that single game, a total of 176 minutes and 30 seconds since the opening face-off. Exactly 116 minutes and 30 seconds were overtime.

Lost in the Shuffle

"Slingin' Sammy" Baugh was one of football's finest passers. He was also a very fine punter. During his career with the Washington Redskins he set a record of 44.93 yards per punt, the best average in the league.

Then one day a rookie lineman named Bob Suffridge taught Baugh a lesson. Suffridge was an All-American at the University of Tennessee. He was drafted by the Philadelphia Eagles. And when the Eagles played the Redskins, he cramped Baugh's style.

Three times Suffridge broke through the Redskins' line and blocked punts by Sammy Baugh. It was a truly remarkable feat, but there were no headlines for Suffridge.

That game was played on December 7, 1941—Pearl Harbor Day. That was the day the Japanese destroyed most of America's Pacific fleet, bringing the United States into World War II. The papers had much more important news to print.

Lonesome Runner

In the early years of the Olympics the rules were made and enforced by the host country. It was assumed the host would be impartial. Unfortunately, during the 1908 Olympics bitter feelings developed between the Americans and their British hosts.

The feud probably began when England neglected to display the American flag among the others brightening the stadium, claiming they couldn't find one. The Americans retaliated by refusing to dip their colors in tribute as they paraded by King Edward. "This flag dips to no earthly king," said discus thrower Martin

Sheridan. The Swedish flag too was not displayed. Later Sweden withdrew from the competition after a disagreement with the British rules-makers over a wrestling event.

There was much bickering between the English and Americans throughout the games. Things came to a head in the 400-meter run. Among the runners were three Americans: J. C. Carpenter, J. B. Taylor, and W. C. Robbins. The English entry who had a good chance to win was Wyndham Halswelle.

In the final 100 meters Carpenter, Robbins, and Halswelle were grouped together. Carpenter and Robbins were on the inside. Then at the last turn Carpenter cut in front of Halswelle, taking the lead. Instantly the British officials began to shout, "Foul! Foul!" They claimed that Carpenter—deliberately, according to their view—had interfered with Halswelle. One of the judges ran onto the track to stop Taylor, the other American. Another judge cut the tape before the race was over. The order of finish was Carpenter first, Robbins second, and Halswelle third.

After some deliberation the British judges ruled that the race was void. Carpenter was disqualified for a foul. The other three—Taylor, Robbins, and Halswelle—would have to run the race over again.

Carpenter protested that he had done nothing wrong. He always pulled out wide during a race. Halswelle could have passed on either side of him if he'd had the speed and stamina left to do so. "We just raced him off his feet," Carpenter declared. "He couldn't stand the pace."

American officials also protested, but the British refused to change their ruling. Fuming, the Americans withdrew Robbins and Taylor from the rerun.

Two days later Wyndham Halswelle was the only entry in the 400-meter run. He had the track all to himself as he ran the distance in 50 seconds. Mostly because of that controversy, from then on international judges supervised Olympic events instead of the host country.

SHOOTING YOUR AGE

In golf "shooting your age" means that a golfer will take as many strokes over an 18-hole course as his age. Therefore, when an 80-year-old golfer cards 80, he has shot his age.

The oldest golfer ever to achieve that feat was Mr. C. Arthur Thompson of British Columbia, Canada. In 1973 he played the Uplands course, which is 6,215 yards. At the time he was 103 years old, and he shot 103.

Scoring Spree

Most hockey games have low scores, especially in Olympic hockey. No team really wants to humiliate its opponent. Sometimes, however, a team is so inept that nothing can be done. It would be even more humiliating if a team deliberately refrained from scoring.

That was the situation the Canadian skaters found themselves in during the 1924 Olympics. Their opponent, Czechoslovakia, had a defense as porous as a sieve. The Canadians won, 30–0. Harry Watson of the Canadian team scored 13 goals. Although official records for individuals in Olympic hockey are not usually kept, according to the Hockey Hall of Fame's annual guide, *Hockey's Heritage*, Watson's scoring spree is the Olympic record for a single game.

Arguing with the Umpire

Back in the 1950s a gentleman named Jack McKeon was the player-manager for Missoula, Montana, of the Pioneer Baseball League. McKeon, a funny fellow, enjoyed needling umpires because he knew the fans liked to watch him argue with the officials. In one game he almost drove umpire George Sosnak crazy with a whimsical prank.

McKeon was catching, and he accidentally tipped the batter's bat as he swung. Sosnak called interference and awarded the batter first base. McKeon knew he had been guilty of interference, but he heard the fans booing the call and decided to have a little fun.

The catcher ripped off his mask and snarled at the umpire. "That was a good call, George. I certainly did tip the bat!"

The umpire wasn't sure he had heard what McKeon had said. The catcher continued with the charade, much to the fans' delight. He waved his mask, kicked the dirt, and stuck his face against the umpire's.

"I said it was a good call!" he yelled. "You're right, I did interfere with the batter."

The umpire stared blankly, then said, "Are you feeling all right, McKeon? Are you sick or something?"

"I sure am!" McKeon began to stamp his feet in mock anger. "Can't a guy have a little fun for the benefit of the hometown fans?"

The bewildered umpire tried to turn away, but McKeon followed him around in circles, still acting to entertain the fans. The booing grew louder.

"McKeon, do you want the fans to kill me because you're having fun?" asked the disgusted umpire.

Now McKeon began to tear at his hair. "They won't hurt you, George," he assured the arbiter. "Don't be a spoilsport. Let's have some laughs."

Finally Sosnak had enough. "McKeon, you quit clowning this minute or I'll throw you out of the game," he warned.

"You can't throw me out for saying you made a good decision," McKeon retorted.

"I'll toss you out for delaying the game," Sosnak threatened.

McKeon returned to his position reluctantly. The Missoula fans never did learn what McKeon had said to the umpire.

The Retriever

Joe Kirkwood was one of golf's most famous trick-shot artists. During his exhibitions Kirkwood would use weird looking clubs that he designed himself. Often the clubs would get as big a laugh as his unusual shots.

Joe ran away from home at the age of nine and worked for J. R. D. Sellers, a sheep rancher. To while away the hours he practiced playing golf on a three-hole course that was on the rancher's property. He had a sheep dog, which he trained to retrieve balls.

It was while he was still very young that Kirkwood began to experiment with different types of shots. He hit the ball left-handed and right-handed. He would hit it standing first on one foot and then the other. Pretty soon he had mastered all sorts of trick shots. But he practiced golf seriously too.

Mr. Sellers liked to play golf and he encouraged the youngster. When Kirkwood was about 12 years old, Sellers sent him to a town about 30 miles away so that he could participate in a tournament.

Young Joe went to the first hole, teed up, and drove off. Sure enough, his sheep dog ran out and retrieved the ball. The tolerant officials allowed Joe to leash the dog and start all over. He won the tournament by seven strokes.

High and Low

Cy Young won 511 games during his career, more than any other pitcher in major-league baseball. But he lost 315 games, which is also more than any other pitcher in the major leagues.

THE BIG APPLE WAS FIRST

Sports programs are among the most popular shows on television. Games are watched in virtually every home in America. And it all began in New York City.

On May 17, 1939, the first baseball game was televised. It was a college game between Columbia and Princeton, played at Baker Field in New York. The first football game on TV was played at Randall's Island, New York, on September 30, 1939. The participating teams were Fordham and Waynesburg College. On February 25, 1940, the first hockey game was shown. Madison Square Garden was the site; the teams were the New York Rangers and the Montreal Canadiens. Madison Square Garden hosted the first basketball game on TV three days later. It was between Fordham and Pittsburgh.

"On Trial"

Leonard Patrick "Red" Kelly, who played in the National Hockey League from the 1940s into the 1960s, was one of hockey's greatest stars. He was also the victim of one of the funniest practical jokes in all of sports.

Red was involved in a minor automobile accident. It wasn't a serious case, but he still had to go to court. Several of his Detroit Red Wings teammates, including Jack Stewart, accompanied him. Stewart volunteered to act as Red's lawyer.

Red should have known something was wrong when Stewart insisted that the jury be made up of 12 old ladies. Then, when the judge entered, Stewart began to "defend" his client by telling enough lies to send the bewildered Kelly to prison for the rest of his life. The judge listened with a frown on his face.

Finally Red caught on. The Red Wings players had framed the whole thing and the judge was in on it.

Red's "fine" was two goals, which he was ordered to score as soon as possible.

Lots of Room

The largest playing field for any ballgame is the one for polo. The maximum allowable length is 300 yards, and the maximum width is 200 yards. Therefore, a polo field can cover a total of 12.4 acres.

The Disappearing
"Kangaroo"

In 1896 a young Australian named Patrick John O'Dea came to the United States and enrolled at the University of Wisconsin. As a teenager back home, he had been a good swimmer and sprinter, but he had never seen a football game. Yet he tried out for the Wisconsin foot-ball team and made it.

There never was a kicker like Pat O'Dea. It was nothing for him to drop-kick a 60-yard field goal. His punts went into orbit; once he kicked one *more than 100 yards on the fly!* With those great legs, and because he hailed from Austra-

lia, he was nicknamed the Kangaroo. He became one of the first football players known throughout America. His fans—and *everybody* was a Pat O'Dea fan—gave him no peace. Wherever he went, he was asked for his autograph. People just wanted to touch him or hear his voice.

His fame did not diminish after he graduated. O'Dea couldn't go anywhere or do anything without being mobbed. Finally Pat O'Dea just vanished.

Nobody knew what had happened to him. Was he kidnapped and held for ransom? Did he leave the country secretly? Was he dead and buried somewhere?

Seventeen years after he disappeared, Pat O'Dea was found. He was living in a small town. He had changed his name to Charles Mitchell. His neighbors hadn't known who he really was. O'Dea explained that he had run away because he wanted to live a quiet life, which was impossible under the name Pat O'Dea.

Once his identity was revealed, Pat O'Dea became famous all over again. For the rest of his life he remained one of America's greatest football idols.

Shine 'Em Up

Nippy Jones had been a baseball player for a long time. He had played first base for the St. Louis Cardinals and the Philadelphia Phillies, but a back injury and an operation put him back in the minors for a while. The Milwaukee Braves brought him back to big-league ball again. He was used mainly as a pinch hitter. Occasionally he filled in at first base.

The Braves won the National League pennant in 1957 and faced the New York Yankees in the World Series. The Yanks won two of the first three games. In the fourth game New York was leading, 5–4, in the bottom of the tenth inning, and Milwaukee's chances looked dim.

Nippy Jones strode to the plate as a pinch hitter. Yankee pitcher Tommy Byrne delivered a low pitch that appeared to bounce in the dirt. The ball rolled all the way to the wall.

"That ball hit me!" Jones shouted to the umpire.

"I didn't see it," replied umpire Augie Donatelli.

"Sure it hit me, I can prove it," Jones said. He got the baseball and showed it to the umpire.

"I shined my shoes before the game," Jones said triumphantly. "Look at the ball and you'll see that it hit me."

Sure enough, there was a smudge of black shoe polish on the baseball. Donatelli awarded Jones first base, where he was replaced by a pinch runner. Then Johnny Logan hit a double to tie the game, and Eddie Mathews hit a home run to win it.

How strange that a shoeshine helped Milwaukee win the fourth game of the 1957 World Series. The Braves went on to become world champions that year.

About the Author

Howard Liss has written for young people more than sixty sports books as well as books on geography and science. He has also written adult novels and nonfiction.

Mr. Liss began his career as a comedy writer, thinking up jokes for such comedians as Eddie Cantor, Al Jolson, Jimmy Durante, and others. He has written successfully for the Broadway stage and for a number of nationally syndicated comic strips. Mr. Liss makes his home in New York City.

About the Illustrator

Joe Mathieu is a popular illustrator of children's books. Among his best-selling titles are *The Olden Days*, *Big Joe's Trailer Truck*, and many Sesame Street books. His recent credits include *A Gallery of Monsters*, *The Book of the Unknown*, and *The Superkids and the Singing Dog*. Mr. Mathieu has also illustrated traditional jazz record albums. He lives in Putnam, Connecticut, with his wife and two children.